JOHN D. MacDONALD

"... keeps one reading with fierce interest."

—*N.Y. Herald Tribune Book Review*

"... is the great American storyteller. McGee is for me!"

—*Richard Condon*

"The John O'Hara of the crime-suspense story."

—*The New York Times*

"An author whose swiftly paced, admirably characterized novels leave you breathless."

—*The Community Reporter*

NOW MEET HIS GREAT CHARACTER: THAT BIG LOOSE-JOINTED BOAT BUM, THAT SLAYER OF SMALL SAVAGE FISH, THAT BEACH-WALKER, GIN-DRINKER, QUIP-MAKER— THAT MAN NAMED TRAVIS McGEE, IN THIS COMPELLING STORY IN THE BRILLIANT SERIES BY

John D. MacDonald

Fawcett Gold Medal Books
in The Travis McGee Series
by John D. MacDonald:

THE DEEP BLUE GOODBYE 14176-4 $1.95
NIGHTMARE IN PINK 14097-0 $1.75
A PURPLE PLACE FOR DYING 14219-1 $1.95
THE QUICK RED FOX 14264-7 $1.95
A DEADLY SHADE OF GOLD 14221-3 $1.95
BRIGHT ORANGE FOR THE SHROUD 14243-4 $1.95
DARKER THAN AMBER 14162-4 $1.95
ONE FEARFUL YELLOW EYE 14146-2 $1.95
PALE GRAY FOR GUILT 14148-6 $1.95
THE GIRL IN THE
  PLAIN BROWN WRAPPER 13768-6 $1.75
DRESS HER IN INDIGO 14170-5 $1.95
THE LONG LAVENDER LOOK 13834-8 $1.95
A TAN AND SANDY SILENCE 14220-5 $1.95
THE SCARLET RUSE 13952-2 $1.95
THE TURQUOISE LAMENT 14200-0 $1.95
THE DREADFUL LEMON SKY 14148-9 $1.95

The Quick Red Fox

by John D. MacDonald

FAWCETT GOLD MEDAL • NEW YORK

THE QUICK RED FOX

ISBN: 0-449-14264-7

Printed in the United States of America.

30   29   28   27   26   25   24   23

A BIG NOISY wind out of the northeast, full of a February chill, herded the tourists off the afternoon beach, driving them to cover, complaining bitterly. It picked up gray slabs of the Atlantic and smacked them down on the public beach across the highway from Bahia Mar. It rattled loose sand across the windshields of the traffic, came into the cramped acres of docks and boat basin, snapped the burgees and went *hoooo* in the spiderwebs of rigging and tuna towers. Fort Lauderdale was a dead loss for the tourists that Saturday afternoon. They would have been more comfortable back in Scranton.

I was cozied up in the big lounge of the *Busted Flush*, my houseboat moored at Slip F-18. My electric heat was turned to high-high. I was stretched out on the big yellow couch and clad in ratty old wool slacks and an old Norm Thompson flannel shirt, faded to a sky blue over the treasured years.

A few days earlier I had junked my old speakers in favor of a pair of AR-3's, and had bracket-mounted them on the far wall. The Scott tuner was locked into WAEZ in Miami, and the Fisher amplifier was driving the new speakers very handsomely. They were broadcasting that Columbia recording of Bernstein conducting the Shostakovich *Fifth*, one hell of a big bold heroic piece of music, and I had the gain high enough to do it justice. You could shut your eyes and float on it.

Skeeter was across the room, hunched over her drawing board. She was wearing gray corduroy coveralls, too big for

5

her. All her clothes always seem too big for her. She is thirty, I think, and looks eighteen. She has cobweb blonde hair, constantly adrift, a Raggedy Ann face, and a narrow graceful immature figure. She is not very well organized, but she makes a pretty fair living doing illustrations for children's books under the pseudonym of Annamara. My friend Meyer found her on the beach a year or so ago. That hairy, ugly, charming fellow can walk down a beach and collect a rare people the way anyone else might pick up a left-handed whelk.

She worked with the top of her tongue sticking out of the corner of her mouth. She was doing line drawings of a dissolute field mouse named Quimby. She was working at my place because they had repainted her apartment three blocks away, and the smell made her nauseous, and she had a deadline to meet. Once upon a time, when I had been feeling shattered by the loss of someone very dear to me, we had drifted sideways into a brief affair. We had found we weren't very good for each other on that kind of basis. We seemed to bring out a talent in each other for chipping away at the weak points. The infighting got a bit bloody, and though we felt obligated to pretend otherwise, it was a relief to both of us to call it off and find our way into a casual and off-handedly affectionate friendship.

At the big parts of the music she would use her drawing pen to help Bernstein conduct, and then go back to mouse work. She had uncovered an unexpected talent for making Navy grog, and I had a mild and pleasant glow from the ones she had fixed me. She had made her own weaker. Quimby demanded her sober attentions.

Into the resonant blare of the music came the frail little overpowered bing-bong of my bell. I have a button board affixed to a dock post, and a chain across the dock end of my small gangplank.

I got up and went and took a look. It was a tall girl out there, a tall girl in a severe dark suit, with a purse that managed to give the same impression as a brief case. She stood erect, pretending there was no wind at all. She looked as if she might be going around enrolling people in a business school. As I peered out at her, she punched the button again. There was no hesitancy about her.

I went out onto the rear deck and up the broad short slant of gangplank to face her across the chain. Her survey of me looked inclusive, and I couldn't tell if she registered approval or disapproval. I get both kinds. I am extra-big. I have been out in the weather. I look lazy and am. In the words of a Texas chick one time, I look as if I had been there and back.

She had black hair. Male musicians often wear theirs longer. She had vivid dark eyes, heavy black brows, a rather long face, high flat cheekbones and a ski-jump nose. The mouth saved the face from austerity. It was full and broad and nicely modeled. She looked fashionable, competent and humorless.

"Mr. Travis McGee?" she asked. She had a furry contralto.

"Himself."

"I am Dana Holtzer. I couldn't reach you by phone."

"It's turned off, Miss Holtzer."

"I would like to talk to you about a very personal matter."

Sometimes it does happen that way. She had a money look. No jewelry. Earned money. She looked handsomely employed, and she didn't look as if she was in any kind of a jam. An emissary for somebody who was. Had she come along a couple of months sooner, I could not have cared less. But the kitty was dwindling. I was soon going to have to cast about for some profitable little problem. It is nice when they come walking up and save you the trouble of looking.

But caution is always essential. "Are you sure you're talking to the right guy?"

"Walter Lowery in San Francisco mentioned your name."

"What do you know? How is old Walt?"

"All right, I expect." She frowned. "He said to say he misses playing chess with you."

So it was all right. Walt and I never played chess in our lives. Not against each other, at least. But that was the identification tag, if he ever sent anybody along. There are the nosy ones, and the troublemakers, and the cuties, and the official investigators. It is good to have a way to weed the doubtful ones out.

"So come in out of the wind," I said, unhooking the chain, rehooking it after she had eased by me. She was long-waisted, with sturdy shapely calves, moving with the grace many women with that kind of build have. Her back was flat and erect, her carriage good.

I opened the door and ushered her into the blast of music. Skeeter gave her an absent-minded glance, a vague smile, and continued her work. I left the music on and took Miss Holtzer on through the lounge and past the galley to the little dining booth. I closed the door from the lounge to the galley corridor.

"Coffee? Drink?"

"Nothing, thank you," she said, sliding into the booth.

I poured a mug of coffee for myself and sat opposite her. "I'm not interested in every little thing that comes along," I said.

"We're aware of that, Mr. McGee."

"You do know how I operate."

"I think so. At least, I know what Mr. Lowery said about it. If something has been taken from someone, and there is no way to get it back legally, you will make an effort to get it back—for half its value. Is that correct?"

"I have to know the circumstances."

"Of course. But I would rather have . . . the other party explain it all to you."

"So would I. Send him around."

"It's a woman. I work for her."

"Send her around."

"That's impossible, Mr. McGee. I have to take you to her."

"Sorry. If she's in enough trouble to need me, she's in enough trouble to come ask me herself, Miss Holtzer."

"But you don't understand. Really. She just *couldn't* come here. She would have talked to you if I could have gotten you on the phone. I work for . . . Lysa Dean."

I knew what she meant. That face was too distinctive, even in the darkest sunglasses in town. She wouldn't want to come on such a private mission with a police escort. And if she came alone, the boobs would recognize her at a hundred paces and come clotting around, pressing in as close as they could, standing and staring at her with that curious fixed, damp, silly smile, America's accolade to the celebrity. Ten big movies, four fairly messy marriages, one television series fiasco, and a few high-paid guest spots had made her a household face. Liz Taylor, Kim Novak and Doris Day would take the same stomping among the star-dazed common folk. The public is an untrustworthy animal.

"I can't imagine Lysa Dean in a situation where she thinks she'd need me."

I thought I saw a little glimmer of distaste on the rather

somber face of Miss Efficiency. "She'd like to talk to you about it."

"Let me see. Walter did a script for her once upon a time."

"They've been friends ever since."

"Would you say her problem fits into the way I operate?" She frowned. "I think so. I don't know all the details."

"Aren't you in her confidence?"

"On most things. But as I said, I don't know *all* the details of this. It's been a personal kind of thing. But it is . . . something she wants to get back. And it's valuable to her."

"I can't promise anything. But I'll listen to her. When?"

"Now, if you could manage it, Mr. McGee." The symphony ended. I got up and went and turned the set off. When I came back Miss Holtzer said, "We'd rather you didn't mention this to anyone. Even her name."

"I was just going to run out and tell a few friends."

"I'm sorry. I've gotten so used to trying to protect her. She's beginning a promo for *Winds of Chance,* starting Monday. The world premiere will be next Saturday night in eight Miami theaters. We came early hoping for a chance to see you. She's staying at the house of a friend now. She'll move over to the hotel penthouse on the beach tomorrow evening. She'll have a full schedule, starting Monday."

"Have you worked for her very long?"

"Two years. A little over two years. Why?"

"I wondered what you call yourself."

"Personal secretary."

"She tote a big staff around?"

"Not really. On the road like this there's just me and her personal maid, her hairdresser, and the man from the agency. Really, I would rather you asked her the questions. Could you . . . get ready to go see her?"

"In Miami?"

"Yes. I have a car waiting, Mr. McGee. If . . . I could make a call?"

I took her into the master stateroom. The phone extension is in a compartment in the headboard. She looked up the number in a black leather note book from her big purse. She dialed the operator and made it a credit-card call. "Mary Catherine?" she said. "Please tell her that our friend is coming back with me. No, that's all. Pretty soon now. Thank you, dear."

She stood up and looked around the room. I could not tell if the huge bed repelled her or amused her. I was tempted to explain it. It startled me that I should want to tell her that it had been part of the furnishings when I had won the craft in a long poker siege in Palm Beach. The man wanted another advance to stay in the game, this last time putting up his Brazilian mistress as collateral, under the plausible assumption that she too went with the boat, but his friends saved me the delicate problem of refusal by leading him gently away from the game.

Miss Holtzer did not look particularly austere. She just looked as if she might put people in handy categories.

She decided she would pour herself some coffee while I changed, if that was permitted. I put on the very infrequent necktie, and a fairly heavy suit. When we went back into the lounge, Skeeter said, "Hey, both of you look at this lousy mouse a minute."

She showed us the drawing just completed. "This is when Quimby finds out for sure he's really a mouse. That cat just told him. He's crushed. He thought he was a real small pedigree dog. But I think maybe he looks more scared than crushed. When you look at it, is it as if he's scared of the cat?"

"It's absolutely charming!" Dana Holtzer said. "What a horrid thing, really, to find out that all along you've been a mouse."

"Quimby can't adjust," Skeeter said.

They smiled nicely at each other. "Dana Holtzer, Mary Keith—known as Skeeter. We have to run. Skeet, make sure you lock up if I don't get back before you go."

"Sure. What's bugging him is all that trouble learning to bark."

"Forage if you get hungry."

But she was back at work, insulated and intent. Miss Holtzer and I headed into the wind, toward the parking areas. She said, "That's a dear strange girl, and very talented. Is she a special friend?"

"They've just painted her apartment so I told her she could work on the boat. She has a deadline."

Within another three steps, Miss Holtzer had tucked the escaping loose ends of personality back into her executive secretary shell. I had a memory of how pleasure in the mouse had brought her alive, younger and surprisingly more vivid. But it was not in her manner or habit to give anything away. She would do her job, reserved, armored, efficient. She was not being paid to react to people, nor to show her own reactions, if any.

A glittering black Chrysler limousine was waiting, tended by a middle-aged man in dove-gray uniform with silver buttons. He touched his cap and opened the door for us. He looked like a television U. S. Senator. And he had that uncanny ability of the skilled chauffeur to drift a big car through traffic with such rhythm that the bunglings of other drivers seemed like an untidy and unimportant mirage.

"Miss Dean's car?" I asked.

"Oh, no. It belongs to the people where we're staying."

"When did you get in?"

"Yesterday."

"Incognito?"

"Yes."

"That's a good trick."

"Chartered airplane," she said.

There was glass between us and the barbered neck of the skilled driver. Her face was turned away from me, looking placidly out at the gray day.

"Miss Holtzer."

"Yes?" she said, turning with polite query.

"I'd like to know if I am right or wrong. I get this impression of quiet disapproval."

I thought I saw a flicker of bleak amusement. "Is that sort of thing so important to you, Mr. McGee?"

"I've never thought so."

"Mr. McGee, in the past two years I've been sent on so many curious errands, I would have become quite worn out if I'd tried to make value judgements about them."

"Then you avoid having opinions?"

"Except where it is expected of me. She pays for opinions, Mr. McGee. Legal opinions, tax opinions, artistic opinions. She listens and makes up her own mind. She doesn't particularly care for volunteer opinions."

"And the job pays well?"

"It compensates me for what I do."

"I guess I better give up."

With an almost imperceptible shrug, she turned again to

look out her window, presenting me with the nice modeling of the strong line of her throat, the neatness of an ear set into a casualness of cropped black curls, a fringe of black lashes visible beyond the smooth line of her cheek, a faint and unobtrusive and understated fragrance of mild perfume.

two

THE HOUSE was on a private island, over a small causeway from one of the main causeways between Miami and Miami Beach. A gardener swung the ornate gate open for us. We turned into a winding crunch of gravel between lush and carefully tailored jungle, rounded a buttress of pink and white stucco, parked in a small walled area by a garden.

It seemed to be a back stairway. Miss Dana Holtzer led me up half a flight and into a shadowed hallway. I sat on a Babylonian throne under a black gleam of hanging armor. There was no sound in the house. None. She came back, hatless and purseless, and beckoned to me with all the gravity of a head nurse. I followed her down a paneled and carpeted corridor. She rapped on a fortress door, pushed it open for me and stood aside, saying, "She'll be with you in a moment."

She closed the door and left me alone in what seemed to be a guest suite. I was in a long room with a high ceiling. Plum carpet. Paneling. Seven arched windows along one wall, high narrow windows with leaded panes, deep sills. Black Spanish furniture. The center portion of the room was sunken. At one elevated end was a canopied bed. At the other end was an elevated portion with a conversational grouping of furniture around a small slate fireplace. The sunken portion was furnished in rather formal fashion. On the bed level there were two doorways. One, ajar, opened into a dressing room area. I could see pieces of matched luggage in there. The other door was closed, and I could hear an almost inaudible whisper of running water.

Though the draperies of all the windows were pulled aside, the room was not particularly bright. I went to a window. Tropical trees shaded it. Looking down I could see patches of shaded green lawn. Off to the left, through foliage, I could see one bright corner of a white swimming pool.

The bathroom door opened suddenly and Lysa Dean came out. She was not smaller than I had expected because I was prepared for a woman smaller than she had looked to me on the VistaVision Screen, in living color, in close-up, each slanty gray-green eye as large as a Volkswagen sedan. She came across the bedroom elevation and down the three steps toward me. She made the absolute most of those three steps. She wore flat sandals with gold straps. She wore faun-colored pants in a fine weave. They fitted as tightly as pants, or paint, or a tattoo, could fit. She wore a strange furry blouse, with a big scooped neck and three-quarter sleeves. It looked as if Skeeter's Quimby and a couple of hundred of his relatives had contributed their pale belly-fur to this creation. Around her slender throat was knotted a narrow loose kerchief of green silk precisely matching the single jewel she wore, an emerald as big as a sugar cube on the little finger of her left hand.

She came swiftly toward me, hand outstretched, her smile full of the warm delight of a woman welcoming the returning lover. "So good of you to come!" she said in her light, breathy, personal voice. As I took her hand she turned slightly so as to face the bright and shadowed daylight. It is the most cruel light a woman can accept. Her hand was small and dry and warm, a trusting little animal as intimate as her voice.

They have the distinctive occupational tricks. A lot of expressive business with mouth and eyebrows, animation with gestures.

I could remember, quite vividly, a long conversation with a stunt man named Fedder. Arthritis had forced him out of the business.

"Don't let anybody tell you they're not worth the effort," he had said. "A lot of them aren't. You got to look close to see which type. They all have to be damned good-looking and well-built. So suppose you get a chance at one who's a pretty good little actress. Let it go. The thing there, they sublimate. That's a word I learned once. They take all that steam and they shove it into their work and there isn't enough left over for bed. Now suppose you got one *thinks* she's a hell of an actress, but she's a ham. You skip her too. She'll take all that ham to bed with you and be so damn busy watching herself go her heart won't be in it. The ones to wait for, and go a long way out of your way to get, they're the ones that plain started off with such damn good glands they don't have to do any acting. The camera picks up how good they'd be. Man, they can't rest from tracking it down and trying it out. The next one is always going to be the biggest and best yet. They've got what you call a real strong interest."

I had the feeling Fedder would approve of this one. I had not expected her to have such a genuine flavor of youthfulness. By every way I could measure it, she had to be about thirty-three. Yet she was a young girl, and not in any forced way. She had the slimness, the clear-eyed look of enormous vitality, the fine-grained and flawless skin, the heavy swing of burnished hair. Her impact, so carefully measured it seemed unaffected, was of a kind of innocence aware. A gamin sparkle, hinting at a delicious capacity for naughtiness.

But I had known enough of them to know that this was but one role. The enticing woman who is not in the industry will have five or six faces to wear. One like this would have dozens, and this was the one she had momentarily selected for me.

She had the showbiz trick of close-range conversation. Normal people keep their faces a yard apart. Eight inches is the focal distance on the Coast. Eight inches keeps you aware of the girl-breath heat against your chin, and the upthrust breast-bud an inch and a half from your chest.

"Any friend of Walt's . . ." I said inanely.

"I treasure that man." She backed away a quarter step to give me a cock of the head and an urchin appraisal. "He said you were big, but he didn't say how huge, Travis. Trav? He called you Trav, I think. I'm Lee to my friends. Dear Trav, he told me you were big and rough-looking and sour and sometimes dangerous, but he did not tell me you are so terribly attractive."

"A veritable doll," I said.

"It's so wonderful of you to agree to help me."

"I haven't."

She was quite motionless for a thoughtful second, her smile in place. The capped teeth gleamed, between moistness. Green of iris speckled amber near the pupil. Delicate geometry of the hairs of red-gold brows. Fantasy length of the darker lashes. Faintest of fuzz on her upper lip. It was an unusual and grotesquely familiar face, the features slightly sharp, extremely sensuous, unmistakable. With her head slightly bowed, looking up at me through her lashes, the gold-red weight of hair at the right side of her face had swung slightly forward. Suddenly I knew what she reminded me of. A vixen. A quick red fox. I had seen one in heat long ago on an Adirondack morning in spring, pacing along well in front of the dog fox with a very alert and springy movement, tail curled high, turning to see if he still followed, tongue lolling from between her doggy grin.

She turned abruptly away, walking toward the elevated part of the room where the chairs and fireplace were. "But you will help me," she said in a small voice.

I followed her. She sat on a small couch and pulled her legs up. She took a cigarette from a table box. I held the light for her. She huffed smoke from the delicate oval nostrils of the slightly pointed nose, and as I sat in a big chair half facing the couch she smiled across at me. "You are refreshing, Trav McGee."

"How am I managing that, Lee?"

Her shrug and laugh were self-deprecatory. "You don't say what I always hear. I loved you in this. I adored you in that. I see every picture you make. You look better off the screen than on, actually. You know what I mean."

"I'll go through all that when I ask for the autograph."

"You know, you are sour, aren't you? Or are you afraid of seeming to be impressed. Or don't you give a damn? It's a little unsettling, dear."

"Your Miss Holtzer unsettled me the same way."

"Dana is a gem. When she reacts, she lets you know it."

I shrugged. "I loved you in this. I adored you in that. You look just fine in person."

Again she was motionless. It was an odd feeling to be so close to her. It made me aware of the uncounted millions of men all over the world who had stared at her image, coveted her, lusted after her, mentally stripped her and plundered those silky little loins. I wondered how many secret, solitary orgasms had been engineered with her in mind. The unmeasurable scope and intensity of all that vast and anonymous wanting gave her a curious physical impact. True, she had spent years being starved, pummelled, flexed, rubbed, plucked, burnished, perfumed and trained into the absolute peak of lovely physical condition. Without a chromium ego and a savage will she could not have endured it so long. But one could also believe that, as sex symbol, she also carried sex to an ultimate otherwise unknown—providing ecstasies unimaginable, greater heats, deeper spasms, longer agonies than mortal woman could know. And this, of course, was the nonsense a man must guard himself against. Her physical confidence, approaching arrogance, would lead the unwary to believe it.

"Excuse me, please," she said politely, and hurried the length of the room, toward the dressing room. A girlish graceful haste, forever eighteen. She came back with a large manila envelope and put it on the table beside the cigarette box.

"That big chest down there is a bar. If you want to fix yourself anything, I would like some of the sherry. Just half a glass, please."

As I walked to the bar, she raised her voice and said, "It is so terribly difficult to know where to start, dear. You don't seem to make it any easier for me."

"Just tell me the problem. You told Walt, didn't you?"

"Just some of it. But I would guess you want to . . . know all of it."

"If I'm to help you."

As I carried the drinks toward her, she said, "Celebrity! If all the ones who'd like to be one only could know what it means. You become such a target, actually. Slimy schemes to fasten themselves onto you for the free ride. You cannot make a single careless move."

This was the new pose. She sipped her wine. I sat down. The suffering celebrity. Public responsibility.

She gave me a sad smile. "It isn't worth it, you know. But you have to get into it as far as I am to realize it isn't worth it. And then it's too late. You can't get out. They still follow Garbo. How long since she made a picture? A thousand years, at least. Oh, there have been some satisfactions, of course. But the things I really treasure—contentment, friendships, peace of mind, marriage—none of those things could survive all the rest of it. There is a terrible loneliness, Trav. Like being on top of a mountain, alone."

"They pay you for it."

"And they pay very well indeed. I've had good advice. I have quite a lot of money. Of course, it is invested in a lot of things, but if I should take it all out, it would be quite a large sum. That's why I did try to . . . buy my way out of trouble."

"Blackmail?"

She put her glass aside and got up quickly, pacing about in an agitated way. "Can you see how valuable it is to me . . . how *essential* to have a little time when I can be myself? Like here with you now. We can talk like two people. I don't have to pose with you. I have to forget sometimes that I am Lysa Dean, and just be plain Lee Schontz from Dayton, Ohio, the fireman's daughter. Sixteen-ten Madison Street." She whirled and stopped with a leg-warmth against my knee. "You can understand that basic human need, can't you?"

"You can't live up to the public image at all times."

"*Thank* you for understanding!"

This was another role. I guessed it was a speech out of an old movie, edited to fit the present need.

"And when I do . . . forget, that's when I'm most vulnerable."

"Sure."

"I *so* want you to try to understand me. I'm not really very complex, Trav. I am the same as everyone. I have times when I feel desperate and self-destructive. I have times when I do foolish things. There are times when I do not give a damn what happens to me."

"Sure."

She reached and drew her fingertips across my cheek and whirled away and sat on the couch again. "I know you're not a prude. I can sense that. This has to be as if I'm talking to my doctor or my lawyer. But I do feel so terribly shy about this."

"What happened?"

She sighed and made a rueful face. "A man happened to me. Of course. He was a very exciting chap. Exciting to me, at least. It happened a year ago last July, over eighteen months ago. We'd just finished shooting *Jack and the Game*. I was literally exhausted, but I went off with Carl.

Carl Abelle. He had a ski school. We'd never had a chance to really be alone. He found a place for us. An absolutely fantastic little house. Do you know California? It was just below Point Sur, and clinging to the rock by its finger-nails. Friends of his named Chipmann own it. They were in Switzerland. They have another house there. It was just the two of us . . ."

Her voice trailed off into uncertainty.

"Yes?"

"Trav, I am under the most terrible disciplines most of the time. I do work very hard."

"So when you let go, you let go?"

"More than most, I guess. Just a little time of not watch-ing every ounce and every quarter inch, every blemish and drink and calorie and bruise . . . God damn it, to be a woman for a change. Fry eggs, let my hair go, get stoned, have a ball. I'm naturally a very passionate woman. But I keep it all under control. Until a time like that a year and a half ago. With Carl. That's what I try to do. Get away like that, with a certain kind of man. Then everything that's been saved up . . ."

"Birds and bees. I didn't think you went into a convent when you had time off, Miss Dean. I don't follow this routine."

"It's just to explain how things happened. It was such a very *private* place. Carl would drive off to buy food and liquor. There were steps cut into the stone, down to a little beach way way down that you couldn't use at high tide. There was a terrace on the ocean side, twenty feet square, about. It was a little offset so you could get morning sun too. A low broad wall around it. And a great stack of weatherproofed sun mattresses and pillows in all kinds of colors. We'd arranged it so we could have three weeks alone. Maybe that was too long. I guess it was. We were marvelously right for each other, in a purely physical way. We knew that before we went there, of course. Except on a ski slope or in bed, Carl isn't very stimulating. It was very intense for about a week, I guess. Day and night all mixed up. Eat when you're hungry, sleep when you're sleepy. When the edge was gone, we both started drinking more. And we spent more and more time on the terrace in the sun. I knew I was getting too brown, but I was too lazy and relaxed to give a damn. I was drinking a lot of vodka. Hot sun and vodka kept me in a sort of permanent daze. We'd make love there in the sun, all slow and sweaty and, I don't know, remote somehow. I had a tube pregnancy when I was just a kid and damned near died and I don't have to worry about taking care of anything. The thing is, we felt so *private*. You'd see a boat way out, or an airplane far away, or hear a truck sometimes on the highway. The phone was cut off. I had a little radio. You have to understand that nothing seemed important, absolutely nothing at all. Do you understand that, Trav?"

"I've been there."

"Anyway, it must have been just about at the end of two weeks, we needed things and Carl drove to town to get them. He left in the early afternoon sometime. And he was gone so long I began to get damned annoyed at him. I belted the vodka pretty good, so by the time he did come back, I was getting kind of sloppy and confused. He came skidding back into the driveway with two cars following him, and the whole drunken bunch came marching into the house bellowing some goddam German skiing song. Five fellows and three girls. He'd known one of the girls up at the Valley. He ran into them in town, and had drinks with them, and decided we should have a house party. They damned near fell over when they saw who his girl was. They'd brought tons of food and beer and liquor and cigarettes from town. I was sore at him, but I thought that as soon as they had recognized me the damage was done, if any, and the hell with it. I guess I was getting bored with Carl and I lost any sense of caution. They were swingers, every one. The girls were darling. The fellows were fun. I guess there's no good way to avoid telling you all, dear. It was a very scrambled evening, all things considered, and by late afternoon the next day the last holdout, the girl they called Whippy, she got tight enough to let Sonny peel her out of her swim suit and get her into the fun and games on the terrace. It just seemed to be a crazy time for everybody, and nobody seemed to care much, and you saw everything and did everything through a kind of sleepy crazy haze so that in my memory it's all jumbled up. It was the first and last time I was ever in a situation like that. It's sort of standard practice on the Riviera, with those car-light signals and horn signals to get recruits and all. It didn't offend me. In some ways it was very exciting. But it was just too dangerous for anybody in my position. And I hadn't *wanted* it to happen. Carl brought them back to the house and it just went on from there, and lasted, oh, four days I guess. When I got back to Brentwood it took me *weeks* to get back in shape. It all seemed like a dream. Then one day toward the end of August I got a big envelope in the mail. There were twelve photographs in it. Eight by ten glossies. There is a great deal of difference between remembering something and seeing it . . . like that. Seeing yourself . . . God! I flipped my lunch."

"It came by mail?"

"Yes. To my home. God only knows how Dana didn't get to it first. There was a note with it. I saved it. I put it in my wall safe. Here it is."

She took it out of the envelope and handed it to me. It was done with a carbon ribbon on an electric machine, with several strikeovers.

"Save the envelope?"

"Not that one. It was mailed at the main post office in Los Angeles. Not special or anything like that. Not even marked Personal on the outside. The address was typed with the same type as that note. No return address. Go on. Read it."

It read as follows: Lysa, dear: You are practical. You know how the industry makes book. So you have no choice, of course. I have ten complete sets of the enclosed and a good idea of how to distribute them. I recommend the investment. Installment plan, ducks. Ten thousand in used hundreds each time. Wrap in plain white paper. Tie securely. Each Sunday night starting a week from next Sunday, you or your dark secretarial type takes a drive. At midnight, precisely, pull into the Narana Kai Drive-in at Topanga Beach. Order something, then walk alone with the packet in plain view, over to the public pavilion. Walk to the far edge of the concrete, next to the public phone booths. A phone will begin to ring. Count the rings carefully. Wait and it will ring again the same number of times. Go back to your car. Leave the drive-in at exactly twelve-thirty. Take note of the exact milage on your speedometer. If it says, for example, eight and six tenths and the phone rang seven times, when the milage ends in five and six tenths, (simple addition, dear) be ready. You will be heading west on 101. Be over in the right lane, your right window open, packet

in your little right hand. Look for a light ahead and off to
the right. Slow to thirty-five and get just as far right as
you can. When you see a little green light blink twice, toss
the packet out onto the shoulder immediately. If it blinks
red twice, take the money home and come back the following Sunday. Each time you will receive the negative of one
picture and all the prints made from that negative. They
will come in the mail. If all goes well, and if you have
no clever and silly ideas, we should be through with this
whole affair in twelve weeks.

"So damned complicated," she said.

"Actually pretty shrewd. Two people could manage it with
very little risk. One at the drive-in and pavilion to check
you or Miss Holtzer out, then after you've heard the rings,
phone up the road for his buddy to get into place at
the designated spot. He gets a chance to see that nobody
is hiding in your car. He follows you out of the lot, tails
you until it looks safe, then passes you and gets there first
and gives a headlight signal to his buddy to use the green
lens on the flashlight. Not bad at all. Very difficult to
trap them. What went wrong?"

"Nothing. At least not then. I paid. One night there was a
red light. I don't know why. It took thirteen weeks. I got the
stuff in the mail. The worst ones came toward the last.
Dana made the deliveries. Her nerves are better than mine,
I guess."

She jumped to her feet, flushing. "Don't be dull, McGee.
Close to seven million went into *Winds of Chance*. Risk
money. The character who wrote that note knows this industry. He knew how I had to jump. It isn't like the old days,
where you could count on studio protection. Each picture is
a separate packaging operation. There are just about ten
men these days who can put the really big packages together. If each one of them got a set of those prints, why
should they take any future chances on me? Those pictures are poisonous. What's a hundred and twenty thousand compared to my potential? I liquidated some holdings
that weren't doing so good, and took my tax loss, and paid
off. Don't tell *me* what I should have done!"

It was a good act and I had to admire it. "How can I
help you if all you give me is a smoke screen?"

"What the *hell* do you mean!" she shouted.

"All the industry cares about is money in the bank. Your

name on a picture puts money in the bank. Just like Liz,
Frankie, the Swede, Mitchum, Ava. They have not been
dear little buttercups all the way. The days of the Ar-
buckle effect are long gone, dear. In our culture there is
going to be no huge concerted public censure to drive you
off the wide screens. If you get a little rancid, the PR people have you endow a dog shelter, and all America loves
you. Drop the act."

The faked indignation was turned off in an instant. She
sat again, looked at me with sullen speculation. "Smart ass,"
she said.

"What is it, then, that made you pay off?"

"A few little things. A while back I swung my weight
around too much. It delayed the wrap-up and bumped the
budget, and some people decided maybe they didn't want
to work with me. But I smartened up and settled down.
I could read what it said on the wall. You know, like
Monroe and Brando. But it left them edgy. Also, there've
been a couple of little things from time to time. Not as
bad as those pictures, but . . . along that line. It just
didn't seem to be the right time to make them feel any
more insecure."

"And?"

"Boy, you really want everything, don't you?"

"I've learned that it helps."

"I have a very dear friend. He's very devout and very
conservative and he owns great big vulgar hunks of California and Hawaii. If he can get the right paper signed by the
Vatican and get loose, I'll never have to take any crap
from anybody again as long as I live. And one of those sets
of prints would have gone to one man who would have
felt obligated to give my friend a look at them. And that
would have torn it."

"So those are the real stakes?"

She moistened her lips. "Under community property, one
half of about eighty million, honey. I am his dear faithful
little darlin'. It made the whole thing a lot more . . .
chancy. Otherwise I would have borrowed some muscle
from an old buddy in Vegas and turned them loose on this
clown photographer. They'd be smart enough to handle that,
but they're not smart enough to handle what I need now.
Actually, if Mr. X had no knowledge of my friend, and
how long it takes to bull something through that Vatican

crowd, he made a very stupid pitch. But with my friend in the background, there was just too much chance it might backfire. Before you bet, you count what's in the pot. All my potential plus my friend's heavy purse. So I paid off."

"And hoped that was the end of it. And it wasn't. Incidentally, can he clear you with his church?"

"I was never married in his faith, so nothing counts. I get a clean bill. By the way, McGee, Dana doesn't know a thing about my plans for my friend."

I asked her how she thought the pictures had been taken. "It had to be a long lens," she said. "You can see the flattening and foreshortening effect. Off to the left, south of the house, I remember a little rocky ridge higher than the house with some knotty little trees clinging to it. It had to be from there. The angles match. But he had to be part mountain goat, and it had to be a tremendous lens."

"Is there any clue at all in that letter itself, any hint that's made you think of a specific person?"

"No. I read it over and over. He's been around the industry in some connection, and I think he tried to sound as if he knew me, but he calls me Lysa instead of Lee. That could be a cover-up, of course. And it has a phoney kind of limey slant to it, calling me ducks."

"What size were the negatives?"

"Little. Like so." She indicated a 35mm frame size.

"You checked them against the prints each time?"

"Sure did. But in a lot of cases the prints were just an enlargement of part of the negative, even less than half sometimes."

"So you were all paid up well over a year ago. And you thought it was over. When was the next contact?"

"Two months ago. Less than that. Early in January. An old friend, trying to make a comeback, was opening at The Sands in Vegas, and a bunch of us were rallying around to give him a good sendoff. It was in the papers that we were all going to be there. Dana was with me. We had a suite at the Desert Inn. Somebody left this envelope for me at the desk at The Sands. I guess they thought I was staying there. They sent it over. Dana got it. I was just waking up from a nap. She came in with the damnedest expression on her face and handed it to me. She had opened it. It was another set of the pictures. There wasn't any return address. The desk had no idea who had left it off. Dana wanted to quit right then and there. She is a strange gal. I had to explain the whole thing the way I explained it to you, Trav. She knew right away that it was the same thing that had cost me all the money. She still wanted to quit. I had to beg her to stay. Our relationship hasn't been the same since she saw the pictures. I don't blame her. I'd still hate to lose her. This is the envelope. You can see how it was addressed. Somebody just cut my name off the front of a fan magazine, something like that. Here is the note that was with it."

It was quite different. Individual words and letters had been cut from newsprint and newspaper stock and pasted to cheap yellow copy paper. It said: Shameless whore of Babylon you will be cut down by the sord of decency and money will not save your dirty life this time but you better have money ready you whore of evil I will come to you and you will no the truth and I will set you free.

She hugged herself. "That one just scares the hell out of me, Trav. It's kind of sick and crazy and terrible. It just isn't the same person. It can't be."

"So you went and saw Walter?"

"No. I just got more and more jittery the more I thought of it. I'm still shook. I was at a big party at the Springs and I got a little stoned and made a scene and dear Walt was there and he took me for a walk. I hung onto him and cried like a baby and told him my troubles. He said maybe you would help. I guess you can say something was stolen from me. My privacy or something. And somebody wants to steal my career or maybe my life. I don't know. I've been carrying cash around with me. In thousand-dollar bills. Fifty of them. I don't expect you to get back what I paid. But if you could, you could keep half. And if you can get that nut off me, you can have the money I'm carrying around."

"Are the pictures in that envelope?"

"Yes. But do you have to see them?"

"Yes."

"I was afraid of that. I am not going to let you see them until you say you'll try to help me. Every time I think of that note I feel like a scared kid."

"It's a very cold trail, Lee."

"Walter said you are clever and tough and lucky, and he said being lucky is the most important." She gave me an odd look. "I have this feeling that my luck is running out, darling."

"How many people know about this?"

"The four of us, dear. You and Dana and me and Walter. But you know more than the other two. Not another soul. I swear."

"Wouldn't it be logical for you to tell Carl Abelle?"

"Sweetie, when one of those things is over, it is over all the way. Enough is enough forever."

"Could he have set you up for it?"

"Carl? Definitely no. He's a very sunny type. Very simple needs and very simple habits. Totally transparent, really."

"Usually I gamble expenses, then take them off the top before the fifty-fifty split. But this is a little too chancy for that."

"Expenses guaranteed up to five thousand," she said without hesitation, "and when that's gone we'll talk some more."

"Walt must have said I could be trusted."

"What other choice do I have? That's one thing about this. There hasn't been any trouble making decisions. There's been just one way to go. Will you try? Please? Pretty please?"

"Until it looks hopeless."

She scaled the envelope into my lap. "God knows I'm not the shy type, sweetie, but I don't think I could watch anybody look those over. I'll take a walk. Take your time."

She went to the heavy door and let herself out quietly.

three

AFTER A LITTLE TIME I put the twelve photographs back into the envelope. I took a slow turn around the room. I am too big a boy to be churned up by the explicits of other people's kicks.

Nor did I feel any compulsion to make moral judgment. These were modern animals caught in black and white at their silly play. Such sport was not for me, and very probably not for anyone whose friendship I claimed. There seemed to be some kind of severe selection involved. An acceptance of that presupposed an inability to accept or believe in a lot of other things. Personal dignity for one.

But something still bothered me, something I could not quite define. So I took them out and shuffled through them again. The clue was there. It was the terrible loneliness on their faces. Each one of them, in all that lazy confusion of intimacies, in that lexicon of clinical descriptions, looked utterly, desperately alone.

And they were beautiful people. Lysa Dean was the featured player in every shot, and her body was as superb as its promise.

I felt as if I had glimpsed the edge of some great paradox. The grotesque ultimate of togetherness is the final loneliness of the human spirit. And once you had been that far out on that barren limb, there was no chance of ever coming all the way back.

I shrugged and looked at them again to see if they told me anything about time lapse. I put them away again.

From the varying lengths of shadow in the pictures, from

the changing positions on the sunny terrace, I could tell that they had been taken over a matter of hours, perhaps on separate days.

Soon she returned, coming in with a look half challenge, half calculated demureness. "Well?" she said.

"It doesn't look as if it was a hell of a lot of fun."

That response startled her. She stared at me. "Oh, you are so *right*! You know, it seems to me as if it was all a thousand years ago. I guess I've been trying to fade it out of my mind. Oh Christ, there's kind of a sickly excitement about it, I guess. But what I remember now is being constantly cross and irritable and impatient. And sleepy. Just terribly sleepy and never being allowed to sleep long enough, and having the feeling that all the rest of them were just one . . . one *thing* somehow. Not like the pictures."

"Are these exactly like the other pictures you got?"

"They are the twelve exact same shots, but not exactly like the others. These are fuzzier and grayer, sort of. Not as sharp. But I didn't save any of the others to compare, of course."

"We have to look through these together so you can give me the names to go with the faces, Lee, and tell me what you know about each one."

"I suppose it has to be done."

"Like a trip to the dentist. I think there's at least one fair picture of every other person in the group."

She made a face. "Those pictures are such a big boost to my pride, Travis. It does something for a girl to look like a fifty-peso floozy in a back-room circus in Juarez."

I turned a light on and we sat at the desk in the sunken part of the room. I found a pencil and paper. I pointed to the pictures and asked the questions. She answered in a thin small breathy voice, her face half turned away. I took the following notes.

1. Carl Abelle—about 27—six-footer—husky—blond— has left the Valley—try Mohawk Lodge near Speculator, New York.

2. Nancy Abbott—about 22—tall, dark, slender, heavy drinker, good singing voice, believed to have been divorced, perhaps daughter of an architect. Took ski lessons from Abelle at Sun Valley. Believed to be a house guest of . . .

3. Vance and Patty M'Gruder, perhaps of Carmel, married couple in middle twenties, apparently well-off, Vance a sailboat buff, ocean racing etc., have house in Hawaii (?), husband very tanned, short, broad, muscular, going prematurely bald, wife lush & fair, very long blonde hair, quarrelsome, strong English accent.

4. Cass—could be first name, last name or nickname. Seemed to have known M'Gruders previously. About thirty. Dark, hairy, handsome, very powerful. Amusing (?). A painter, perhaps. Friend of . . .

5. Sonny, a little younger than Cass, slender, cold-eyed, flavor of violence, untalkative, occupation unknown, who had brought along . . .

6. Whippy. About nineteen then. Copper curls, freckles, perhaps a waitress or clerk, scared of Sonny.

7. Two college boys from the east on a summer trip, apparently joined the group at the bar where Abelle ran into Nancy Abbott. Boys about 20 or 21, Harvey a big blond cheery one and Richie a smaller dark nutty one. Cornell.

On the clearest prints of each I had marked the corresponding number from my notes. I could sense Lee's relief when I put the photographs back into the envelope.

"Who got it all started?" I asked her.

She tightened up again. "Why? What do you mean?"

"I don't think a camera gets that lucky. Somebody had to set you up. Or maybe the real target was somebody else, and you turned out to be a bonus."

"It was a long time ago, and I was tight most of the time."

"Tell me what you can remember of how it got started."

She got up slowly and went over and rested her fists on a windowsill, staring out, the fox-pelt hair softly backlighted. I leaned a shoulder against the wall by the window. She talked. Her voice was small. I could not see much of her profile because of the way the hair swung forward. Round of forehead, soft snub tip of nose. I did not press her. I let her find her own words in her own time. Her memory was more acute as regards textures than incident. Six men and four gals that first evening and night. Four places to go—two bedrooms, a long couch in the living room, the leathery sunpads on the night terrace. It was a prowling thing then, pursuits and tensions, Lysa Dean a primary target for all but Carl, low lights and ultimate arrangements, and some re-pairings when partners slept.

In phrases and fragments, theatrical sighs and beautifully timed hesitations, she painted the flavor of the hot bright terrace on that first full day of houseparty. Pitchers of Bloody Marys, vodka haze, arrows of white sunlight through squinting eyes, compulsive beat of the music on the portable radio, oil and aromatics of sun lotion, jokes and tipsy laughter. A game of forfeits, with the rules rigged so that to play was to lose, and to lose was to soon be naked.

In half-sleep, mildly and amiably drunk, after the game had ended, she had fended off the increasing insistence of Cass, whining at him irritably when he became too bold. Finally, propping herself up to drink again, she saw several sound asleep, and saw others who were accepting what she had refused. So, squeezing her eyes hard shut to achieve the illusion of privacy, she had surrendered herself to Cass and her own responses.

She straightened and turned toward me and hooked the fingertips of both hands into my belt, leaned her forehead against my chest. She sighed and said, "Then I guess it stops mattering so much. I don't know. You just seem to learn how to turn one whole part of your mind right off. It's all just something that happens. Everybody is in the same boat. So it doesn't seem to make any difference any more. Nothing does."

She sighed again. In the cold soft light I could see the scalp, clean and white as bone under the coppery spring of hair. "I don't know who started it. Patty was bossy. I can remember people getting mad. Whippy cried sometimes. Cass knocked Carl down once, I don't know why. One of those college kids, the big one, kept getting sick. He couldn't drink. It's all so vague, sweetie. If you watched, and you were all turned off, it was just sort of stupid and boring, and if you'd started to hum a little, you could get into that one or set up something else, or go take a shower, or go make a sandwich, or go build another pitcher of drinks. It just . . . wasn't all that important."

She slid her small hands around my waist, laid her cheek against my chest and held tight. I stroked her hair. She took the deepest breath of all and said, "Listen to me! God, I know it was important. There are some kinds of poisons,

I heard you look as if you got over it, but you never really do. I wish somebody could stick a knife in my head and cut out those four days and nights, Trav. A girl thinks about herself a different way, after that. I have this lousy dream ever since. I've fallen into this empty white swimming pool and the sides are too high to get out. The pool lights are on so it's bright as a stage. And there are six ugly snakes in there on the tile, all after me. I can run and dodge fast enough to keep away from them no matter how they try to hem me in. They all look exactly alike. Then I keep calling for help and suddenly I see that the walls are all kind of coming in. It is getting smaller and smaller. Then I know they are going to get me. As the place gets smaller the snakes get bigger, and I scream and wake up, all sweaty and trembling. Just hold me tight, Trav. Please."

She was trembling and I wondered if it was faked. After several minutes she quieted down and moved away from me, shoved her hair back with the back of her hand and said, with a funny little shy smile, "You don't want me, do you? I could tell. Just from your hands. Kind of gentle and . . . fatherly and remote. God, I wouldn't blame you for not wanting such a public piece."

"It's not that."

"No? You are certainly not one of those, sweetie."

"No. Well, in all honesty, if that's what you want, I guess the pictures have something to do with it. A man likes the illusion of exclusive option, even on the most temporary basis, I guess. But with or without pictures, let's just say I'm not a trophy hunter."

"What the hell does that mean?"

"Every redblooded American boy should ride a bike no hands and win some merit badges and go to bed with a household name. Some of them don't get over it, that's all. I had my celebrity innings, but I'm not a locker room historian. I outgrew my bike too, Lee. It's a big scene here. Rich silent house and the closed door and your tight pants and that rostrum type bed. And mutual attraction. But it isn't worth it. It would be like being taught to dance by your elder sister. She would keep trying to lead, and giving irritable little instructions, and counting out loud and spoiling the music. Then she would give you a patronizing pat and say you did just fine."

For a moment she had the malignant rigidity of a temple demon. Then an urchin grin, seen often in your favorite movie palace, broke it up. "My God, you *are* a strange one, McGee. You wouldn't want me as a gift, eh?"

"Not unless and until it could be more than this for us, Lee."

"You mean like real true love?"

"Affection, understanding, need and respect. You can be sarcastic about that too, if you want. Bed is the simplest thing two people can do. If it goes with a lot of other things, it can be important, and if it goes with nothing else, it isn't worth the time it takes."

She strolled over and curled up in a big chair and pondered me, finger laid against the side of her small nose. "The next time around, Mr. McGee, can you arrange to show up in Dayton about fifteen years ago?"

"I can make a note of it, Miss Dean."

"I've been through too many mills this time."

"Not necessarily."

"But you said respect."

"Once in a while you stop posing for me and remembering lines from old movies, and then I could respect the person that shows through."

"It could be strange to have a friend like you. I have no female friends, really. And just two male friends, fine old guys, both in their early sixties. I love them dearly. Males in your bracket are either studs or competitors, sweetie, or they want to find an angle to get rich off me."

"We might end up friends, Lee. I better go along. I am going to take these pictures along." As I picked them up from the desk she hopped up out of the chair and came running over and grabbed at the envelope. I did not let her pull it out of my hand. I said, "Either you trust me all the way, or I get off right now, Lee. I need them for information and leverage."

After looking at me with a long and searching intensity, she let go. "I never thought I'd let anybody even see those. Trav, will you be terribly careful?"

"Yes."

"I can send Dana over with the expense money tomorrow. Will that be all right?"

"Fine."

"Please be careful with those pictures. If they get out,

my career is dead right now. And . . . as you must damn well know, it is the only thing I have left."

Tears balanced on her lower lids, and one broke loose and tracked her cheek. It did not look real. A makeup man had darted onto the set and put them there with an eye-dropper. Pure glycerine. Maybe they weren't real. She would have learned to cry almost at will, and cry in a way that would leave her as lovely as before.

"You be careful, Lee. I don't like the sound of that note. Sexually disturbed people try to be the sword of the Lord, going around slaying the sinful. See that you get pretty good protection this week in Miami."

She walked me to the door. She caught at my arm, gave me a quick kiss, as soft and trusting as a child's, then went down the corridor with me, found Dana Holtzer in a small room, typing, and turned me over to her. Dana got up and took me down the stairs and out to the waiting limousine. I saw the quick and wary way she glanced at the envelope I was carrying, and caught a flavor of total disapproval.

The driver's name was Martin. She told him to take me back, or to wherever I wanted to go. It was after five. I had him stop where I could phone. I phoned Gabe Marchman in Lauderdale and told him I had a problem. He said it was convenient to bring it right over.

On one of those hunches that may save your life, though you can never prove it one way or another, I had Martin drop me off downtown. I went into one end of a big drugstore and out the other and into a cab.

Gabe Marchman was a great combat photographer. You have seen his name on those classic Korea things. A land mine smashed his legs all to hell. While convalescing in Hawaii, he met and married a very rich and very beautiful little Chinese-Hawaiian girl named Doris. Gabe looks like a sawed-off Abraham Lincoln. He is still on crutches. They have six kids. With his mobility gone, he has gotten into another aspect of photography. He has one of the most completely equipped private labs in the South, taking up a wing almost as big as the main house. He does experimental work, and problem assignments for large fees. He is a sour little man, adored by all who get to know him.

Doris, blooming large again with child, sent me on through to the lab. Gabe grunted at me. I said I wanted to know as much as possible about some pictures I had with me. We were in his print room. He turned on more intense lights. He levered himself onto a stool and spread the dozen pictures out in a row on top of the work table.

From his lack of reaction, they could have been pictures of puppies or flower gardens. "Whadaya know about 'em?" he said. "Just technically."

"They were taken a year and a half ago in California on 35mm film. The person involved estimates that the only place from which they could be taken was about a hundred yards away, but that is just an estimate. The person involved saw another set of prints over a year ago, and they were just like these as far as subject matter, but these seem to be fuzzier and grayer."

He grunted and got out a large magnifying glass and began to go over them very carefully, one by one.

I said, "I forgot something. My client saw and destroyed the negatives. The negatives included more than in a lot of these pictures."

He continued his careful examination. Finally he swiveled around. "Okay, we accept the hundred-yard distance. I would say it was probably Plus-X using a very fine telephoto lens, one thousand millimeter. Maybe the f/6.3 Nikkor, a reflector type with two mirrors. It's only about so long and weighs three or four pounds. It was used with a tripod or some other kind of solid rest. With 35mm a lens that size gives you about a twenty-power magnification, so at a hundred yards it would give the same as a normal lens fifteen feet from the subject. These three are the only ones where he printed the full frame. Now, if he printed about half the frame, it would be like being seven or eight feet away from the subject. And this is the average for most of these. Just this extreme close-up was done from maybe a quarter or less of the negative, showing the woman at a viewing distance of about three feet, with less definition. There's good depth of field and all motion is frozen, so a hundred yards away I'll buy. Okay so far?"

"Yes."

"Assuming the same guy who took the pictures made the original prints, he's a good workman. Excellent exposure, good edge to edge definition, and when he masked the negatives and did his printing, he had good quality control. You can tell that he did some burning in and dodging, and

he couldn't help using a pretty good sense of composition.
I would say he took a hell of a lot of shots, maybe several
hundred, and came up with the best ones. Very sharp, very
clear, and he made high-gloss prints. I'd say definitely a
pro, if that's any help to you. Now then, some clown got
hold of a set of the prints. See this little flare here on this
one and this one. That's where his lighting kicked back off
the gloss. He made a set of copy negatives and a new set
of prints. This is crappy paper, and he butchered his de-
veloping and butchered his printing solutions and times, but
there was enough quality in the prints he copied so that
all in all it comes through not too bad. The guy who did
the originals would be incapable of doing such cruddy work
the second time around, even if he was operating in a motel
closet. But, having the copy negatives, he can make any
number of these poor prints. Your client destroying the
original negatives means nothing now. It is unmistakably her
in every one of these. I would guess she's the one you're
working for."

"Yes. Now I wonder if you can do something with these."

"I was afraid of that."

"From these can you make another set of negatives, and
a set of prints that are a little different than these?"

"McGee, if you start out with crud, you end up with
crud. I can't get back to the original print quality. I can
print for more contrast and clean up these whites a little,
but a close focus on fuzz gives you fuzz."

After an original reluctance, he began to get interested.
He used a copy camera, a larger negative size, a copy film
with a fine grain. By the time he had developed the negatives, Doris began to howl for a little cooperation, so he
hung them up to dry and we went in for drinks. The nursemaid had taken over the bedtime routines. The older ones
trudged in to say their well-mannered goodnights. Doris
cooked and served an old Chinese-Hawaiian specialty—
broiled steaks, baked potatoes and tossed green salad. The
three of us, in front of the big fireplace with a very small
fire, revamped the State Department, simplified all tax legis-
lation, tore down half of Florida and rebuilt it in a more
sane and pleasing fashion.

Then we went back to work. He would put a negative
in the enlarger and focus it on the base, and I would tell
him what I wanted. Then he would go to work. He would

cut a piece of masking paper to fit Lysa Dean's projected
face. He would use sufficient exposure time to give him
opportunity to dodge and burn in so that the face of someone else was emphasized. I ended up with fourteen useful
prints, on double-weight paper. Some of those that took in
more people were duplicated, altered slightly to highlight one
and then another.

Somewhere in the processing they ceased to have any
fleshy impact. They became problems in light and shade
and emphasis. He put them in his high-speed dryer, and
after he had flattened them in a bonding press, I studied
them under the bright lights. Lysa Dean's features were white
censored patches. Gabe was careful to give me the negatives as well as the test prints which hadn't worked out.
We argued price, with me trying to increase it, and agreed
on a hundred dollars. Doris had gone to bed.

He crutched his way to the door with me, and came out
with me into the cold windy night.

"Taking a little trip, I suppose," he said.

"Yes."

"None of my business. I suppose somebody got too
greedy."

"That's usually the way."

"You watch yourself, Trav. A little animal like that, if
she'd see a way out by pushing you over the edge, she'd
take it. That's an interesting little face, but it isn't a good
face."

The taxi slowed, putting his spotlight on the numbers.
He turned into the drive. When I looked back I saw Gabe
still standing there.

four

WHEN I got back to the *Busted Flush* I saw my lights still on. It was a little past eleven. The lounge door was locked. I went in and found Skeeter sound asleep, face down on the yellow couch in her baggy gray coveralls, one frail long-fingered hand trailing on the floor. Drawings of Quimby were propped everywhere. They were wise and funny and good. I admired them. In the middle of the floor was a big stamped brown envelope and a note to me:

This LOUSY mouse. I am pooped out of my mind. PLEASE would you stuff him in this envelope. He is all weighed in and everything, and PLEASE would you seal him and run him to the P.O. He's an airmail-SPECIAL mouse. Honestly, I had to sleep or DIE!!!!

I looked down at her. It was typical. God knows how long she'd gone without sleep or when last she had thought of eating. Perfectionists who meet deadlines are usually pretty whipped out.

I went through to the bow of the *Flush* and put my dirty pictures in the hidden safe. It might not take an expert all night to open it, but he'd sure raise hell finding it first. I assembled Quimby and sealed him and turned off one of the lights.

She stirred and raised a sleep-bleared Raggedy Ann face, shoe-button eyes peering, cobweb hair afloat. "Whumya timezit?" she mumbled.

I squatted beside the couch. "You eat anything?"

"Huh? Eat? Uh . . . .no."

I knew the problems. I had lived with them. I went into

the galley, picked cream of mushroom soup, opened the can, heated it, poured it steaming into a big two-handled mug. She was gone again. I sat her upright and fitted the mug into her hands. When I was sure she was going to keep on sipping at it, I left and took Quimby to the post office and dropped him into an airmail slot.

By the time I got back, the empty mug was on the floor, and she had sagged off to sleep again. I picked her up. The fool girl seemed to have no substance at all. My guest stateroom would have to serve. I carried her in there and then, instead of dropping her into the bed and covering her over, on a strange and lonely impulse I sat on the bed still holding her in my arms. A faintness of marina lights came through the ports. Water slapped and licked at the curve of the barge hull. Mooring lines creaked.

She put her arm around my neck and said, "I thought we gave up on this."

"We did. I thought you were asleep. Go back to sleep."

"I was asleep, damn it. What's this brooding sorrow bit anyway? It's the tenderness keeping me awake."

"I guess I wanted to hold onto you. That's all. Go to sleep."

"Why should you want to hold me? My God, Travis, we ripped each other up pretty good and got over it a long time ago."

"Why do you have to know everything? That's one of your problems."

"I have to know because I can't go back to sleep, that's why."

"Okay. I don't have too many illusions. I just ran into something rotten, that's all. I don't feel shocked. Just sad."

"It was a rotten girl?"

"I don't know. It's a kind of waste, I guess. Go to sleep."

She settled herself more snugly into my lap, arm around me, face in my neck. In a little while she drifted off, and the arm fell away. Her breathing turned deep.

I guess it can be touching. A special kind of trust. Something warm to hold. The way a kitten will drowse in your lap, totally confident.

Holding something alive, warm, sleeping is like handling fresh moist soil under the sun's heat. Restorative.

After a little while I had the idea that it would be an act of good fellowship to peel her out of those coveralls and slip her into the bed. A nice gesture. Sure. This is how McGee kids McGee.

I gave a little shake like a hound coming out of water. During that little time when it had been good, before we had started sawing chunks off each other, I had discovered that narrow little body to be amazingly strong, curiously luxurious. And I had the lonelies.

So I stood her on her feet and held her until she could stand up. "What the hell!" she said.

I stood up and kissed her, gave her a swat on the fanny and told her to sleep tight. I heard the coverall zipper before I got the door entirely closed behind me.

I showered with the strange feeling I was washing off the sweat and sunoil I had acquired on a bright terrace three thousand and more miles away.

I put on a robe and went topside for a nightcap pipe, a load of Irish aromatic in a battered old large apple Comoy. I perched a haunch on the sundeck rail. The wind had died, but the surf still made that endless freight-train sound on the beach. Across the way the Alabama Tiger's perpetual floating house party was muted down to a few girlish squeals and somebody playing bad bongo. Meyer's craft was dark.

Go mention it in the locker room, McGee. There you were with Lysa Dean, and she had on these skin-tight pants, fellas, and there was that big damn bed over there, and her hanging on me, sighing. Go on, McGee. Go *on*, man!

Boys, once when I was riding my bicycle no hands, I hit a stone and removed about one-half a square foot of hide from assorted painful places. And once upon a time I won free dancing lessons from Arthur Murray because I knew, right off, what happened in 1776.

When I got up in the morning Skeeter was gone, leaving the bed unmade and no coffee in the pot. But she left a drawing on the sink in the head. A rangy mouse who looked extraordinarily like me sat holding a Skeeter-like girl mouse asleep in his arms. The caption said, "Notorious mouse spares innocent prey. Vitamin deficiency suspected."

After breakfast I phoned her. She said her apartment was smelling much better, thank you.

"McGee," she said. "We might be turning into friends. That's pretty good, don't you think?"

"You're too dangerous on any other basis. What's with this vitamin gag?"

"I guess I was just sort of asleep. You started breathing hard. Then pow! On your feet, girl. And you went off like you used starting blocks."

"Friends play fair, Skeet."

"Well, hell. I don't know. I hadn't decided. You were blue. I practically had a band-aid complex. Woman's work or something. I passed the buck by sort of sleeping. Anyway, I was terribly tired."

"Quimby is a fine mouse."

"Trav, dear, I am going to sleep for three days, and then you can take me fishing."

"Deal," I told her. She hung up. It was a sad thing that we had a strange sexual antagonism that made us want to chop each other to bits. We had to cut deep to see how much it would hurt. And it hurt aplenty. You can't live with that. But you can learn to live very nicely without it.

At eleven o'clock Dana Holtzer, as carefully poised as an unfriendly diplomat delivering an ultimatum, arrived with the money. Five thousand in cash. She had a receipt form for my signature, made out in the form of a letter of intent. The money was for "expenses in connection with research for a moving picture as yet untitled, to be purchased in treatment form at a price to be negotiated. . . ."

Apparently I was dealing with something called Ly-Dea Productions. She had a file copy of the letter for me. She sat erect on the cushioned top of one of the stowage lockers along the lounge wall under the ports. She wore no hat. She wore a tailored navy blue suit with pleated skirt over a crisp white blouse. I could see no concession to anything in the set of her heavy mouth, the waiting attentiveness of very vivid dark eyes. Had I not seen her reaction to Skeeter's mouse, I would have given up on her.

"Tax reasons," she said.

"Of course," I said, and signed her copy. She refolded it briskly and tucked it away.

I wondered if anything would dent that efficient calm. I expected her to get up and trot off. But she had something else on her mind, yet wanted me to make a move first. I could guess why she had no particular enthusiasm for me. Her confidence would be given to large organizations with computers in the airconditioned basement to tell the other machines which cards to drop into the slot. Lysa Dean was in trouble. When you are in trouble, you go to J. Edgar Hoover, not to an obviously shopworn beach bum, a marina gypsy, a big shambling sharpshooter without an IBM card to his name. To Miss Holtzer I would look like more trouble, not less. My khakis were faded to pale beige, and the toes were out of my topsiders, and the old blue sweatshirt was fringed at the elbows. So I just fell into a chair, hooked a leg over one arm of it, and watched her mildly.

She took it well and took it long, and then the pink climbed up her throat. "Miss Dean should be the one to tell you this," she said.

"Tell me what, dear?"

"She could answer any objections better than I could. The agency is sending a competent girl out, to take over for me temporarily with Miss Dean. I'll catch her up to date this evening." She took a deep breath. "Miss Dean has assigned me to work with you on this matter, Mr. McGee."

"That is absolutely ridiculous!"

"Believe me, it wasn't my idea. But in all fairness, it does have some merit. I can get through to her immediately at any time. There may be information about her you might want to have, and information about her friends and associates. Also I may be able to take some details off your hands, travel arrangements, accommodations, notes, financial records. Miss Dean would feel . . . more at ease about all this if I am with you."

"I work alone, Dana. My God, I don't need any Katie Gibbs-type services, believe me. I wouldn't know how to act with you trudging behind me with a note book and a ledger. In a thing like this I might have to do a lot of . . . impersonations."

"I am quite flexible and resourceful, Mr. McGee."

I stood up. "But you don't belong in this sort of thing. It looks as if it would be pretty messy, if I have any luck at all."

"I said yes to Miss Dean, but I do have one reservation. I must ask you if . . . if you are employed to kill anyone."

I boggled at her. "What?"

"That's a risk I wouldn't care to accept."

I sat down and I laughed. She let me laugh it out, without a smile, with quiet patience. When I was through she said, "That's answer enough. I had to ask. I have to think of risks."

"Miss Holtzer, I don't know if I could stand the continuous weight of your disapproval."

"What does that mean?"

"I understand you saw those pictures by accident, the ones left at the desk at The Sands, and you wanted to quit then and there. Life is full of a number of things, Miss Holtzer, and many of them get a little grim from time to time."

Her dark eyes flashed. "Do they really?"

"Haven't you noticed?"

With a thoughtful expression she took cigarettes from her purse, snapped her lighter, huffed a dragon-plume of smoke toward me. "What I tell you now is, of course, none of your business. But I think we should understand each other a little bit in the beginning. My personal life is out of bounds for any future discussion. I am in the business of selling skills, tact, great energy, adequate intelligence and total loyalty. I sell this package to Lysa Dean for fifteen thousand dollars a year. Assigned to you, you get the same package. When I saw what those pictures were, I went through them to see how damaging they might be. I read the note. To me it meant that Lysa Dean was not as good a gamble for me as she used to be. I worried about that before, when I went through that thirteen-week charade."

I saw her hand tremble slightly as she lifted her cigarette to her lips. "I am married, Mr. McGee. Or was married. My husband was epileptic. He was a talented writer, with a few very substantial television credits. Marriage was a calculated risk. We had a child, a boy. At first he seemed quite normal. Then we learned gradually that he was so seriously retarded an institution would be the only answer. It had no connection with my husband's difficulty. We had to get away after we put the little boy in. He would never know us, or anyone. Bill had made a good sale. It was a good trip, actually, as good as two emotionally exhausted people could expect. We got well enough to head home. We stopped at a place at night for coffee, along the road. It was a bar. We were not drinking. Bill had a sudden seizure. They never lasted long, but they were quite violent. An off-duty police officer thought he was a murderous drunk and shot him in the head. He did not die. He is permanently comatose, Mr. McGee, with tubes for feeding and elimination, and the alcohol rubs to keep bed sores from rotting him away. It is a medical miracle, of course. That was four years ago. I need that fifteen thousand. It is barely enough for me and my family. If Lysa Dean is going down the drain in a messy way, it is my responsibility to leave her before it happens and go where an equivalent job has been offered. The job might not be open if I was in any way connected with scandal. Yes, Mr. McGee, the world can get a little grim from time to time."

"What can I say?"

"Nothing, of course. I thought it would be easier to tell you now before you said more things you might regret later, that's all. You haven't hurt me. I'm not certain anything could hurt me, actually. I am sorry it is all so soap opera. I haven't the . . . self-involvement necessary to make moral judgements. Lee was terribly foolish. The pictures offend me because they are vulgar. And they endanger me. If you can't work things out for her, I will have to leave her. I think she senses that."

"Maybe you could be some help."

"Thank you."

"Drink?"

Her smile was small, and perfectly polite, and totally automatic. "Bourbon, if you have it. Weak, with lots of ice and water."

I do not think she wanted it, but knew I wanted a chance to pull myself together, get the taste of my own foot off my front teeth. I had looked at that empty reserve and guessed repression and disapproval. She was merely burned out. Wires had crossed and a lovely machine had fuzed and quit, become a useless lump for her to carry around the rest of her life. I felt like a jackass adolescent who'd tried to tell a dirty joke in front of real people.

When I went in with the drinks, she was standing with her back to me, feet apart, sturdy calves braced, fist on a rich curve of Mediterranean hip, head cocked, looking at a painting.

"Like it?"

She turned with a swift grace. "Very much."

"Syd Solomon. He lives over in Sarasota. It's part of a Bahama series he did a few years back."

"It's very rich. Are you a collector?"

"Sometimes. I've got about five things aboard and maybe a dozen in storage. Every so often I switch them around." She sipped her drink. "Is that all right?"

"Yes. Thank you. What do you drink? What is that?"

"Lately Plymouth gin on the rocks with two drops of bitters." I could almost hear the little click as she filed that away. I had acquired a drinkmaker.

She went back to the upholstered locker and sat and said, "By the way, my expenses won't come out of what I brought you. Is there anything I can start doing today? My desk is fairly clean and the girl won't be in until later."

I left her there and went to the safe and took out the envelope. I put Lysa Dean's pictures back in the safe and brought out the ones Gabe had made. I handed them to her. She looked at three of them, and then looked at me with faint surprise and fainter approval. "You had this done, or did it, since you left her yesterday?"

"I had it done."

"It's quite clever. I see, I think, what you have in mind. These are no danger to her. Are the others safe?"

"Yes." I waited until she had glanced through the set and put them aside. "Would you take down a few things?"

A note book, gold pen and attentive expression appeared with impressive speed. I gave her Gabe's full name and address. "Make out a check for a hundred and mail it to him for the photo work. The checkbook is in the desk drawer over there. See if you can get a line on a Carl Abelle, possibly a ski instructor at the Mohawk Lodge in Speculator, New York, previously at Sun Valley. Phone him and fake it so that he won't be left with a lot of curiosity. If he is there, find the best way to get there, and reserve us through for Tuesday."

"To stay at that lodge?"

"Let's save that until we get a look, if he's there. Next, see what you can dig up about a Mr. and Mrs. Vance M'Gruder. Their home could be in Carmel. Ocean racing type. It's a small fraternity, so it shouldn't be rough." I went over and sat beside her and handed her my notes. "These are the names and numbers of all the players, as much as she could remember." I identified them in the pictures for her. "All clear?"

"Yes sir."

"Yes, *Trav*. Can we do it that way, Dana?"

"Of course, Trav."

"When will you get loose?"

"Actually tonight, about midnight. The new girl is taking my accommodations at the Sultana at Miami Beach. Suppose I check in Monday morning with you right here. Nine?"

"Make it ten. Or you can come right here tonight when you're through. There's an extra stateroom. With a lock on the door."

She nodded. "It would be simpler. Lock or no lock, Trav, that's one problem I don't expect to have, and know how to handle if I do."

I went to the desk drawer, tossed the extra key to her. She caught it with a deft twist of the wrist. I explained it was to the lounge door, in case I was asleep when she got in. I took her on the tour. She said it seemed very comfortable. I was glad that with a morning attack of the neats, I had made up the Skeeter-tossled bed afresh. She went to the galley and rinsed her glass and set it out to dry. She went to my desk, wrote Gabe's check, altered my dwindling balance, and presented me the check for signature, saying, "Perhaps you would like me to deposit some of that cash tomorrow? I made a note of the account number."

"Half of it, I guess. Thanks. Remind me tomorrow."

I was asleep when she arrived. The little bong of my warning bell alerted me. When anybody comes aboard it rings. Once. That is always enough. I hate unfriendly surprises. I had left a light for her. Gun in hand I prowled naked to the interior door to the lounge, opened it an inch and looked through, out of darkness, saw her open the door, reach back and get a big suitcase and come in with it, moving quietly. It was ten of one. I went back to my bed, behind the closed door to the master stateroom.

She was a quiet woman. A thread of light appeared under my door. In time I heard water running in the head. The thread of light went out. Soft click of latch of the other stateroom. Night silence. A faint music from some other boat. Grumble of a truck on the drive. Distant whistling scream of a jet.

A woman aboard, quite unlike any I could remember. This was a staunch one. A lot of people can be gutsy when there is a tiny morsel of hope. Damn few keep plugging when there is none. The human animal is basically selfish. Neither the damaged kid nor the lost husband could know what degree of care they were getting. Society could not let them perish if she ceased her support. They could not accuse her. But she had a moral obligation so strong, any other course was inconceivable to her. They were her family. There was no other consideration for her. Life had burned her out, but what was left was considerably more woman than was Lysa Dean.

The night thoughts of Dana Holtzer depressed me. Self-evaluation. It is the skin rash of the emotionally insecure. I felt as if I had spent a lot of years becoming too involved with some monstrously silly people. McGee, the con artist. I would fatten myself off their troubles, and then take the money and coast for a time, taking my retirement in early installments. I was not a very earnest nor constructive fellow.

But, I thought, what are the other choices? I am not a nine to five animal. I cannot swallow the myths which say that nine to five is a Good Thing because that's the way nearly everybody else gets stuck. I cannot be an orderly consumer, with 2.3 kids and .7 new cars a year, and an after-hours secretarial arrangement. I am not properly acquisitive. I like the *Busted Flush*, the records and paintings, the little accumulations of this and that which stir memories, but I could stand on the shore and watch the whole thing go glug and disappear and feel a mild sardonic regret. No Professional American Wife could stomach that kind of attitude.

I went to sleep feeling critical of the restless animal called Travis McGee, and awoke to the sun-brightness of nine in the morning coming through the small shaggy draperies in the stateroom, awoke to a scent of coffee, and some furtive clinking sounds from the galley.

After I showered, I went out to find her as full of utterly impersonal morning cheer as a waitress in a good hotel. She said she had slept well, thank you. It's a lovely day. The wind has stopped. It's much warmer.

She said she had taken a chance on the eggs. I said scrambled was just fine. The juice was cold, coffee fragrant, bacon crisp, eggs medium. She served us in the booth. It was a pleasure to watch her move. She gave no impression of haste. Yet each movement was sure, and flowed into the next one without hesitation, and so things got done with a fascinating quickness.

She was wearing gray flannel slacks and a yellow sweater. She looked better in slacks than I would have guessed. She did not look really good. That long-waisted figure was a shade too hearty in the seat and hefty in the thigh to look splendid in slacks. Venus de Milo would have looked like hell in stretch pants. They look just fine on the gangly just-ripening teenagers, or on the calculated slimness of a Lysa Dean. But there is something forlorn and slightly touching about the rump of the mature female who fills them all too well. Dana could not have managed stretch pants, but she did sneak by with the beautifully tailored slacks. They were high-waisted enough to fake a little figure correction, and she was wise enough to wear sandals with about an inch and a half of heel to get her center of gravity a little further from the deck.

As we sat eating our breakfast, I could see why she was worth a lot of money to a Lysa Dean. She had the deft knack of fitting herself to every situation and operating efficiently with a minimum of fuss. There was no sycophantic flavor about her. She knew her own dignity.

I told her about the *Busted Flush* and how I had acquired it. It is one of my more polished routines. I don't expect people to roll on the floor, but I generally get a little more amusement than I got from her. Her laugh was polite and came in the right places.

Over coffee and cigarettes, the little note book came out.

"I had a chance to spend quite a bit of time on the phone, Travis. Carl Abelle is at the Mohawk Lodge. He operates their ski school on some sort of franchise arrangement, and runs the ski shop. It would be impossible to stay there. They are booked completely. If you want to go there first, we are reserved out of Miami to Kennedy, arriving at two-fifteen tomorrow. There is a feeder flight which will get us to the Utica-Rome airport at four-ten. It is about a sixty-mile drive from there to Speculator up Route 8, and the roads are clear."

"What do you mean, *if* I want to go there first?"

"Let me tell you about the others. The M'Gruders are divorced. I couldn't locate her. He has remarried, just a short time ago. They've gone cruising down the Pacific coast to Acapulco, and it is possible they may be on their way back by now. I think I will be able to get a line on his ex-wife. But, having a little extra time, I thought I would see what I could find out about Nancy Abbott. Your notes said her father might be an architect. I checked standard reference sources and found a West Coast architect, Alexander Armitage Abbott in San Francisco. I have a friend in San Francisco, one of Bill's old friends actually, who knows everyone. The architect has a daughter named Nancy, age 24, with matching physical description, so it must be the same one. She has had one annulled marriage. She is a problem drinker. She has been in so many messes, the family has sort of washed their hands of her. He said he would make a couple of calls and phone me back. He did, and said she is in Florida, at some sort of voluntary alcoholic retreat down at Bastion Key. It's called Hope Island. Do you know about it?"

"I took them a customer once. I took her back there three times, but it didn't stick. The same guy may still run it."

"A Mr. Burley? I looked it up."

"That's the one. He gave it a good try with my friend. But she borrowed a car, finally, and drove it into a cypress swamp at about a hundred miles an hour."

"I wondered if . . . as long as she's so nearby . . ."

"Right. We'll go down there tomorrow. Cancel us out on the flight north, and don't set it up again until after we've seen her."

"You have a car?"

"In a manner of speaking. After you left yesterday I was wondering what you think of all this."

"I thought I made that clear."

"I mean what do you think of it as a woman."

"Is that pertinent?"

"Perhaps. It might help me in talking to the Abbott girl."

She thought for a moment. It was a long strong face, flat planes in the cheeks, very dark and vivid and lovely eyes, a prominent and forceful nose, broad firm mouth.

"I would say this, I guess. Lee isn't a suggestible child, you know. She's had four marriages. And other relationships, some of them not particularly wholesome. But she's always been pretty cautious. She is very frankly and happily promiscuous, but the situation in those pictures I would say is not her natural style. She was lulled into it somehow, and damned uncomfortable about it later on, and still is. I wouldn't know how those other females reacted to it. But I don't think it is accurate to think of Lee as just another woman getting involved in something messy."

"What do you mean?"

"She is a property, Trav. She has few personal rights and privileges. She's just worth too much money to too many people. They can't afford a blemish on her. I've gotten used to thinking that way about her. So when I look at those pictures, I see them in terms of risk. Like watching a clown juggle priceless glassware. Those men were aware of it, of course. The unattainable goddess suddenly right there within reach, tired and drunk and sweaty and willing. They talk, you know. It spreads like ripples. It has had a lot of time. Little hints and rumors are coming back home to roost. She's scared of that, too. She'll be all right until one picture doesn't pay off. Then there could be some reluctance. Why take a chance?"

"How will this picture do, this *Winds of Chance?*"

"Very well, I think. It's the kind of part she always does well. Coffee?" -

"Thanks."

After she poured it she hesitated by the table, empty pot in hand. "You didn't say anything about how you'd like me to dress, Trav. I thought. . . . I imagine women have stayed here with you. I'd be less conspicuous if I . . . stayed with resort clothes."

"You do fine. Use your own judgment."

five

ON THE WAY down to Bastion Key, Dana was delighted with
my stately and ancient pickup truck. It is painted a hideous
electric blue and called Miss Agnes by all who know her. It
is one of the largest of the old Rolls breed, and some owner
of long ago, perhaps after bashing her up, did a backyard
job of converting her into a pickup truck. She is high and
solid. It takes a long time to move her up through the gears,
but when you have a chance to get her up to eighty, she will
settle into it all day long in a rushing ghastly silence. She
eats gas, but holds a little over forty gallons at a time.

I liked Dana's delight. It reminded me of the way she
reacted to Skeeter's mouse. I knew I had to watch it, or I
would be trapped into the hopeless project of trying to find
ways to delight her, to bring out that little spark so deeply
buried.

At Bastion Key you turn right off the highway beyond the
town and follow a shell road out to a little short causeway
that leads over to Hope Island. It is not a luxurious retreat.
Stan Burley is the Schweitzer of the gin bottle. The buildings
are surplus barracks he barged in long ago. He and all of
his small staff are reformed drunks. If he has room, he takes
you, at whatever you can afford to pay. He has some the-
ories. They work for him. If you took a seven-foot chimp
and shaved every hair off and painted him pink, you'd have
a recognizable version of Stan Burley. His graduates who stay
dry send contributions regularly.

Before I could turn the motor off, Burley was striding toward us from his little screened office. It was warm and

bright, eleven o'clock on Tuesday morning. The Florida bays were blue.

"Ho, McGee," he said, hand outstretched toward me, looking with a keen expectation at Dana, doubtless thinking her a new guest.

I introduced them and said quickly, "We've come down to talk to one of your people, Stan. If possible. Nancy Abbott."

The welcoming light went out of his face. He gnawed his lip. "Miss Holtzer, you go wait in my office a minute, and Jenny will give you a nice glass of iced tea." She nodded and walked away. Burley led me over to a wooden bench in the shade.

"What's it about, Trav?"

"She was involved in something a year and a half ago. I want to ask her some questions about it. Is she all right?"

He shrugged. "She's dry, if that means very much. Has been since October. I shouldn't tell you a damned thing about that one. But you worked so hard with me that time with Marianne. God help us, we fought hard, but we lost that one, boy. I'll have to tell you, it's on my conscience having her here, this Nancy. It isn't the place for her, but no place is, not any more. Did her father send you?"

"No."

"A retired policewoman delivered the child here in October. Sick drunk and down to ninety pounds. The D.T.'s and the spasms. Pitiful. I got a thousand then, and I get a thousand a month from a San Francisco bank. I write the bank a condition report once a month. After we began to bring her out of it, she puzzled me. I had a doctor friend look her over. Drunk is only part of it. But the thousand a month takes care of a lot of other ones. I'm an evil old man, Trav."

"What's wrong with her?"

"Physically she's as healthy as an ox. She's only twenty-four. She had nine years of drinking, the last five of them heavy, not long enough to damage her. Mentally, you name it, she's got it."

"She's mad?"

"Boy, she isn't sane. What they did, they got too eager with her long ago. Some people who thought shock treatments were the answer to all. A cure for anxiety and depressive symptoms. As far as I can figure, she had over twenty complete series. That and the alcoholic spasms, there's degenerative damage. She doesn't track too well. She can't handle abstract concepts. She's trapped in a manic-depressive cycle. You hit her at her best. She's on her way up now, but not up too high yet. This is her happy time. She could manage in public pretty well if too much wasn't demanded of her. Pretty soon she'll get real wild. Violence, compulsive nymphomania, such a craving for drink she'd kill to get it. Then I put her under restraint. Then she falls all the way down to the bottom. She won't speak for days. Then she starts to slowly build again."

"How is her memory?"

"Sometimes good and sometimes gone."

I looked at that tired simian face and remembered the way he had talked of Marianne. Of love and destruction.

"What did it to her, Stan?"

"Her? The father did it. The adored, talented, mighty father. It was an ugly marriage. The poor child was too much like her mother, so the father couldn't help despising her. He rejected her. So because she couldn't understand why— just like Marianne—she grew up with a conviction of her own worthlessness. Ah, that's where the compulsions start, McGee. A person can *not* endure inexplicable worthlessness. So they establish the pattern of proving themselves worthless. For this child it was sex and drink. The guilts made her emotionally unstable. She was after destruction. The shock treatments and the spasms have done the job for her. She's a destroyed personality. Where can she go? Nothing much can be done for her now. Here is as good as anywhere. Sometimes she is very sweet."

"I don't want to upset her."

"What do you want to ask her?"

"If she can remember some names. If she can remember some pictures being taken."

"Pictures?"

I opened the envelope, sorted out two of them and handed them to him. His face puckered with concern and sorrow. "The poor kid. See what she's saying, in effect? Love me, love me. Rejection by the father, rejection by the young husband, a butchered abortion, a year in an institution when she was seventeen, for hit and run."

"What would showing her these do?"

"Trav, nothing can do her much good or much harm."

"Will she talk to me?"

"In this part of the cycle she's very outgoing. She might get agitated. It might strike her as funny. I don't know. It might accelerate this phase of the cycle. I can't see as that would do any harm."

"Should you be there?"

"I think you'd get more out of her alone. When there's two people or more she wants to be entertaining. She reacts too much. She talks better to one. My God, boy, those are some pictures! A year and a half ago? I guess she was bad off then, but it would take a trained man to see it. Now anybody can see it."

"What's the best attitude toward her, Stan?"

"Just natural, friendly. If she says nutty things, just steer her back to what you want to talk about. Don't look shocked and don't laugh. We're used to Nancy around here, and every drunk in the world has heard everything there is to hear. Treat her as if she was . . . a bright, sweet, imaginative child."

"Where is she?"

He took me over to the office and pointed. "Go around the dining hall and the path to the beach starts on the other side of it. I saw her heading that way about twenty minutes or so ago."

I heard her before I saw her. It was a narrow beach, more shell than sand. It was a lovely contralto voice, very rich and full, singing, with maximum feeling, that cigarette commercial about filter, flavor, flip-top box. She was sitting on a palm log about a hundred feet up the bright beach from where the path exited. As I walked toward her, she heard my steps crunching the shell, stopped singing, turned and stared at me, and then stood up and came toward me with a warm and lovely smile of welcome, teeth very white in her sun-darkened face. "*Hello* there!" she said. "I'm Nancy. Are you one of the new ones?"

She wore pale blue Bermudas, and a man's white shirt with the tails knotted around her waist. Her dark hair was in braids. She was tall and lithe, and her eyes were a dark clear blue. After a mental hesitation, I realized she made me think of Jane in the very oldest Tarzan movies. She was barefoot, unwincing on the shells.

"I'm just visiting. My name is Trav."

"Are you visiting Jackie? She doesn't throw up as much. Maybe she can go home. Just to visit."

"As a matter of fact, I'm here to visit you."

All the warmth and light went out of her face. "He just sends people. Tell him I don't give a damn. Not now. Not ever. Screw him. Tell him that."

"Nobody sent me. I just know some people who know you. I was down this way. So I stopped in. That's all, Nancy."

"What people?"

"Carl Abelle. Vance and Patty M'Gruder."

Scowling, she turned away from me and went back and sat on the log. I followed and stood near her. She squinted up at me. "I know that Carl. A strong back and a weak mind, believe me. He had that stupid idea. The perfect orgasm. Can you imagine? Maybe he thought it worked me up. Damned coward. Too scared to light a fire in that line shack. My God it was always cold in there, way up on that ridge, with Auntie thinking I was on the slopes all day. He stole a key from the office. Fifty dollars a day she was paying him for personal instruction. We'd pile everything on that bunk. What was he trying to get? Tell me that? You either come or you don't. Right? And I almost always do, no matter how quick they are the first time. Last week or last year I was trying to remember Carl's name. My God, he was beautiful on skis. When we'd leave that cabin he'd push me down in the snow and rub snow on my face to get me all pink and outdoorsy-looking, and then guide me down the slopes, all the way to the lodge, half stoned on that brandy, like dreaming and floating. But he said some real dumb things. What was I then? He probably told you. Nineteen? I guess so. I'm remembering better. You ask Stan. He'll tell you. But what good is it? I mean some of the things you remember. Sit by me. But please, I don't want to talk about those puke M'Gruders. I don't have to, do I?"

"No."

"What have you got there?"

"Some pictures."

"May I see them, please?"

She held them in her lap. She looked at them slowly and solemnly, one by one. I watched her face carefully. She sorted one onto the top. She stroked a thumb along the line of Sonny's back. "Burned, burned, burned," she said softly.

"Sunburned?"

"Oh no. He hit a wall. It was his supercharged Merc with special cams and like that. I wore the big red hat so he could spot me, and I sat on the wall by the pits that day. We towed that car all over everywhere, and it burned him up in Georgia. It bounced and bounced." She stroked her thigh. "Sonny liked me in whore clothes. He bought them all. Tight short skirts and tight bright sweaters, and he said I had to swing it when I walked. Proud as a rooster, and mean as a snake, Sonny was."

She ran her thumb across his image on the photograph. "This one right here. Sonny Catton. He took me along when the party pooped out. I was with him maybe two weeks, and he kept beating me up, for taking another drink, or somebody making a pass at me, or sometimes just from re-membering things from the party. Like this picture here, me with this one. What was his name? Cass? Cass something. He drew funny pictures of people. He gave me one of me and I lost it. You know, I've lost every single goddam thing I ever owned? I got sick of him hammering on me and I went home and what do you know, my fa-fa-f-f . . . the man who married my mother, *he* had pictures like this. He said tell my friends it was no sale. They could publish them in the *Chronicle*. Boy, what a smack across the face he gave me! His face was like a stone. I guess it bugged him to see pictures of his wife laying people. Wife! Did you hear that! I'm his d-d-daugh-daughter. Made it!"

My skin had the cold quivers, just below the nape of my neck. "What did you do then, Nancy?"

"Are you another doctor? For a thousand years I've been up to my hips in doctors. I was a woman when I was four-teen, and when I got caught doing it, that was when they sent me to the first one, and I could tell he would have liked it too, if he could get up the nerve. He used to get sweaty and clean his glasses and walk around. They all make a big thing out of stuttering when I try to say . . . ef aye tee aitch ee are. Are you going to give me tests?"

"My name is Trav. I'm not a doctor."

"Trav. Trav, why did he tell you to bring me these pic-tures? They aren't even the same. There were more of me. Hey, you know who this was? This one with no face? A very famous movie star. Lysa Dean! Honestly, I'm not kidding. She's just a little thing, but so gorgeous."

"Who took the pictures?"

"How should I know? I didn't know *anybody* took any pictures until I walked into his study and he had them. He gave me money and I caught up with Sonny again. I was with him a long time. Months, I guess. All over. Wherever he raced. I remember the day he died and the next thing I remember is in the hospital in Mexico City. *Somebody* had to take me down there, but who? I couldn't have *wandered* down there, could I? Somebody dumped me in the hospital parking lot in the middle of the night, I found out later. I had bronchial pneumonia and two broken fingers. I was hallucinating and I had a dose of clap. When I could tell them who I was, they wired . . . him. As soon as I could be moved, he sent people to bring me back and put me in . . . Shady Rest? Refuge Mountain? One of those crappy names. How do you expect me to remember. I can't even remember being brought *here*!"

"How did your father get those pictures anyhow?"

"How do I know? He thought I knew all about it. He thought it was friends of mine, and we cooked it up to get money out of him."

"This is a pretty good place to be, Nancy."

"I guess so. I guess I like it. Sometimes I get very very nervous. After that I get sad. I'm sad a long time. I hum sad songs all day without making a single sound."

"Did anybody at that house party say anything about pictures of Lysa Dean?"

She turned toward me with an exasperated look. "You know, you get to be a terrible bore about those pictures. No. Nobody said anything. I didn't see a camera. Let's drop it, shall we?"

I put the pictures away. "Why are you mad at the M'Gruders?"

"I don't want to talk about it."

"Then we won't."

"You know, you are terribly nice, Trav." She smiled at me, all abeam with innocence. She put her hand on mine.

"Thank you. You're a nice girl."

"I'm a slut, darling. I'm a drunk and a slut. May I ask you a very personal question?"

"Of course."

"Why don't we go over in the bushes a minute, sweetheart?" She tugged at my hand quickly and strongly, trying to press it against herself. I yanked my hand away. "It keeps me from getting nervous," she said. "Please, honey. Please, please, please."

I stood up quickly and she jumped up to try to press herself against me. I held her off with my hands on her shoulders. She dipped her head sharply to the side and licked my hand.

I shook her. "Nancy! Nancy! Cut it out!"

She shuddered, smiled sadly, backed away. "It never makes any difference to a man. Why should you care one way or the other?"

"I have to get back. It was nice to visit with you."

"Thank you," she said politely. "Come and see me again." She squared her shoulders like a child about to recite. "When you get back there, tell my f-f . . . tell him I am being a good girl. Tell him that . . . I am getting good marks."

"Of course."

"Goodby."

I walked the hundred feet to the entrance to the path. When I turned and looked back at her, she shook her fist at me and yelled, "You ask that Patty M'Gruder why she kept locking me up! You just ask that goddam bitch!"

Halfway back to the compound I stopped in the path and leaned against a tree. My knees felt strange. I lit a cigarette, took one drag and threw it away. Stan Burley was in the small office talking to Dana. He got up and brought me some iced tea and said, "How did it go?"

"I don't know. Her memory was pretty good. It damned near broke my heart listening to her trying to call him father. What's the matter with that son of a bitch? He threw her away. He threw away a pretty good person, I think."

"Was she any help?"

"I don't know. I have to check it out. Stan, she made a hell of a direct pass at me."

He raised his ridged monkey brows. "Little early for that. I'll start keeping a close watch on her. Thanks."

"What's the prognosis?"

He wiped his hand across his face. "I don't know. The highs don't seem to get any higher, but the periods of apathy seem deeper and seem to last a little longer. And when she comes up out of them I have the feeling . . . there's a little less of her. She's lost some songs she knew a month ago. She's getting a little more awkward and untidy feeding herself and caring for herself. I . . . I guess we'll keep her here as long as we can. She loves the beach so. She hates to be locked in. This place has the illusion of freedom. Maybe a big institution could arrest it, even improve her a little, but never enough to let her out into the world. She isn't dangerous to anyone. She's a victim. He made her a victim."

"What happened to her mother?"

"She died in a hotel fire when Nancy was seven. She was with a lover at the time. Nancy has a strong body. I am afraid it will keep going long after the brain is gone. Maybe for another forty years or more. There is a brother. Older, and from all reports, extremely righteous. Nice to see you again, Trav. Nice to talk to you, Miss Holtzer. It's a strange world, you know. We can defend ourselves from our enemies, and even from our friends, but never from our family. That tyke was sent to boarding school at age seven. She had lovers at fourteen, alcoholic dementia in a mild form at fifteen, and her first shock treatments at sixteen. I am off to paint chairs. My cure for depression and indignation. Come by any time, either of you."

We stopped at a fish house in town for lunch. We had the privacy of a corner booth. I told her about the dead one. Sonny Catton. I told her about the eight pictures, the slap, the hostility toward the M'Gruders, her final strange comment.

"From the way you look it was rough, Travis."

"I guess so. I don't know why it rocked me so. I guess because she looks so fresh and clean and bright. I guess a man gets the feeling . . . a lovely mixed-up girl, if you could take her along, love her, treat her well, she'd shape up. But you know you can't. Maybe the last one to be in a position to do anything was Catton, but he wasn't the type for it. I guess she got handed around quite a bit, with none of them doing her much good."

I told her about Carl Abelle. The corners of her strong mouth turned downward in an ironic smile. "The Galahad of the slopes. I met him once. I'd been working for her just a matter of weeks. It was quite a while later they went off to stay in that Chipmann house. He was pretty gorgeous.

Dark blond curly hair, huge shoulders, bronzed face, custom sports coat, silk ascot, and a little faky German accent. Hair a little much over the ears. You know. A little wave there too. Lots of huge white teeth, and a very Continental handshake. The almost too typical Hollywood stud."

"Smart enough to rig a blackmail thing on Lee?"

"Oh, I doubt it. I doubt it very much. It couldn't have been his idea in any case. Somebody could have bullied him into it. I think he would shatter quite easily under pressure. Only a damn fool would have tried to use him that way. He would crack too easily. And it wasn't a fool who arranged it all."

"Have any ideas?"

"Who there had money or reputation or something to lose? Lee, and the architect's daughter, and the M'Gruders. Cass apparently, and Sonny and Whippy and the college boys and Carl would be very small fry, not worth the effort compared to the others."

"Agreed. Keep going."

She shrugged. "There's nowhere else to go. We know that two out of the three were contacted. Lee paid off. Mr. Abbott apparently didn't. And we'll know about the M'Gruders later on. We should go to San Francisco, I imagine. After Abelle or before?"

"After."

"Tomorrow?" I nodded. She slid out of the booth. "I'd better do some phoning right now then." She walked to the cashier for change.

When we got back to the boat, Dana checked her copy of Lysa Dean's promo schedule and found that Lysa would be starting a rest hour in about another fifteen minutes. She waited twenty minutes and phoned her on a private line that did not go through the hotel board. They talked together for about fifteen minutes. Then Dana called to me, holding the phone with her palm over the mouthpiece.

"She wants to talk to you. I've caught her up to date on all of it."

When I spoke to her, Lee said in a lazy drawl, "Sweetie, how do you like the little giftie I sent you?"

"I beg your pardon?"

"The highly efficient tragic figger, stupid."

"Oh fine, just fine."

"She'll keep you honest and keep you scrambling, dear. I miss her already. Little things are starting to get fouled up. So don't keep her too long."

"I didn't make any request, you know."

"Oh, don't be stuffy! And by the way, McGee, don't waste your time in any idle hopes. She's quite something in a sort of swarthy hearty way. The look of banked fires or something. Some of the greatest experts in the industry have taken their Sunday hack at that, dear, and wandered glassily away with icicles forming on their whatsis. It is sort of an in-group joke."

"I'm laughing myself sick."

"You are really a wretched chap, aren't you? Why do I still like you? I understand the Abbott girl is out of the ball park."

"Did she seem odd to you at the time?"

"Not particularly. She kept belting herself pretty good, so who expected too much sense? And she was pretty rowdy now and again. Roughhousing into other people's little games. She kept talking about her dear daddy. And singing that song at very strange moments. My Heart Belongs to and so forth. When you see Carl, dear, grasp his hand, smile, give him my love, and kick him solidly in the jewels. I would pay a small bonus for that."

"Just one thing. Is that little accent of his genuine?"

"God, no! It's for the ski trade."

"Are you getting good protection?"

"So far it looks fine. Take care of yourself. Dana will keep me informed."

"Want to speak to her again?"

"Goodby and love to you both. Happy hunting."

I hung up and said, "You plan to keep her informed?"

She had taken the check book from the desk drawer to post the cash deposit she had made. She looked over at me, one dark eyebrow lifting slightly. "In that business, she's so used to intrigue. Everybody watches everybody. And if you work *for* somebody you have to be at a certain established level, a pecking order. She's just trying to fit you into the ranks, Travis, somewhere between a script writer and an associate producer. She doesn't know it won't work, but there's no point in . . . in making a point of it. I'll tell her what she should know, and enough to keep her happy, and no more or less than that. Okay?"

"Divided loyalty?"

"Not really. You are both after the same thing, aren't you?"

"Should that be a question?"

"Mr. Burley told me about a girl named Marianne. I don't have as many questions about you as I used to."

"I'm reasonably honest, Dana, in my own way. That's about as far as I can go with it. Maybe I have a price. Nobody's come up with just the right amount yet. But maybe next time. Let's see how quick you can get us out of here, Efficient Girl."

six

SHE MANAGED to switch it to earlier arrangements on Wednesday. By noon, in a gray February world, we had come down through snow flurries to land at Albany, and had taken off again. When the snow ended the sky was a luminous gray. I looked down at the winter calligraphy of upstate New York, white fields marked off by the black woodlots, an etching without color, superbly restful in contrast to the smoky, guttering, grinding stink of the airplane clattering across the sky like an old commuter bus.

Dana seemed pensive. She had tilted her window seat and had her face turned toward the window, and I could not tell whether her eyes were open or closed. I looked at her still hands resting in her lap, against the nubbly fabric of her suit skirt. You look at hands long enough, you can turn them into animal paws. Her hands were a little larger than perhaps they should have been, the fingers very long and firm, the nails oval, quite narrow, convex. The pads of fingers and palm were heavy. The backs of her hands were very smooth and youthful. You look at hands as animal paws, and you think of the animal aspects of the human, and suddenly you are back on that Pacific terrace, seeing that final and most dangerous form of gluttony.

Perhaps, I thought, the most absolute way of categorizing people is by what they are capable of, and what they are not capable of. Temptation does not deliver most of us into evil, because temptation is a constant and evil is a sometime thing with most of us.

So far I had seen only two people whose pattern of life

had led, almost implacably, toward that terrace. One of them had been on exhibition all her adult life, driven by restless greed, emotional instability, a desire to be noticed. Her artificiality had made this just another act, not particularly real to her while it was happening. The younger one had become food for Jack London's Noseless One long before Abelle and the M'Gruders led her onto that terrace. It, like Mexico, like the tour with Sonny Catton, was just another part of the self-destruction.

I would never talk to Catton. Perhaps it had not mattered a damn to him one way or the other. For the soul to be offended it must first exist. Perhaps to snake-mean Sonny, broads were broads were broads, and if they came in a bundle instead of in separate rooms, he could not care less. He had brought one along and discarded it for one that suited him better. Perhaps for him it was like an exchange counter.

I could not be Sonny. I had the old illusions, including the one that maybe I might be gaining a little bit, just a very damn little bit, in wisdom as my time went by. And wisdom says there are no valuable goods on the bargain counter. Wisdom says the only values are the ones you place on yourself. And I have locked myself into this precarious role of the clown-knight in the tomato-can armor, flailing away at indifferent beasts with my tinfoil sword. A foible of the knight, even the comic ones, is the cherishing of women, and perhaps even my brand of cherishing is quaint in this time and place. Though I have faltered from time to time, I do want the relationship, if it does become intimate, to rest solidly on trust, affection, respect. Not just for taking, or scoring, or using, or proving anything. That knocks out group adventures right there. Not for recreation, not for health rationalizations, not for sociologically constructive contacts. But because she is a woman, and valuable. And you are a man, and equally valuable. There are more than enough girls and boys around. Break down, McGee. Say it. Okay, for love and love alone. They are people, goddam it, not pneumatic, hydraulic, terrace toys. Not necessarily Heloïse and Abelard, Romeo and Miss Capulet, or even Nappi and Joe. But just a crumb of some kind of love there, lad. Love that makes her sweet to hold, warm to murmur to, after there's no more fireworks left in the park. And you can't do that with a terrace toy.

Dana rolled her head toward me and smiled and said, "I was almost asleep." She put a fist against her yawn. "You know, when you are thinking of something and then it all turns crazy and then it turns real again, and you know a dream got mixed into it."

"Tell me the crazy part."

"It's just plain dull, Trav, really. I was wondering if the car would be there as I ordered, and then suddenly I was remembering the last time you and I wanted a car—we didn't ever, of course—and we walked out and got into it and it didn't have any wheels. You were furious and you kept saying they always did that to us. And I was thinking that this time I would look for the wheels before signing the slip, and suddenly I realized how nutty that was. I suppose some psychiatrist would have a ball with that."

"I suppose he'd say you were realizing I can't get anyplace with you."

I said it off the top of my mind. She looked at me for another moment and then said, too casually, "I guess you could make it mean almost anything." She turned her face away again, and I saw the redness climb her throat and up her cheek, suffuse her forehead and slowly die away. It had been too logical a guess, and she had for a moment accepted it, and then taken the next step of translating what it meant to dream that this time she'd look for the wheels before signing the slip. I realized I had innocently created the sort of awareness which would keep her doubly on guard against any kind of emotional involvement with me, no matter how minor.

She arranged the car while I claimed the luggage. When she got in beside me, she had a marked map in her hand. She showed it to me and said, "Just the general idea. I'll call the turns." A most valuable gal.

"Food?" I asked.

"Woops," she said, and scrambled out and hustled back into the terminal. She came out with new marks on the map, and we went a few blocks out of our way into North Utica into one of those Italian-Tourist-Close-to-Motels enterprises called the Diplomat. It wasn't going to excite any farflung gourmet exclamations, but the shots of anti-freeze were excellent protection against the 35-degree afternoon, the lowering sky, the chill moistness of the air. Hot Italian sausage with spaghetti *al dente* was a similar precaution.

You know how it is. You wonder. We had drifted into a silence not entirely comfortable. I hadn't seen much lift or life in her. If we were going to spend a lot of time together, it could become a drag. So you wonder, and you think something up. When you say it, you more than half expect a totally blank look and some kind of query like, for example, "Hah! What's that?"

So when she just started to wind a fork of spaghetti, I said to her, "By God, Myra, I bet you forgot to turn the thermostat down."

Her fork clattered on the plate and she said instantly, "*I* forgot to turn it down? Frank, dear, it was on *your* list. Remember?"

"Of course it was on my list. I reminded you and crossed it off."

"I'd think that once, just once, you could . . . What was it set for?"

"Seventy-five. What else? Sixty-eight is enough for normal people. *You* have to have seventy-five."

"Oh God, all that lovely oil. Darling, maybe we could phone the Hollisbankers."

"So how do they get in?"

She hesitated a moment. "I have it! With Helen's figure, Fred could slip her under the door."

I broke up. A clear victory for her side. You never know until you try. We laughed like a pair of idiots, and then her very next chuckle turned into a strangled howling sob and she jumped up and fled for the ladies' room, nearby lunch customers staring at her and me. She had finished most of her lunch. I finished mine. I would say she was gone a good ten minutes. When she came out her color was not good. Her fine eyes were red-rimmed. She slipped meekly into her chair. She told the waitress she was finished. Just coffee, please.

"I'm sorry," she said to me. "I didn't expect that. It got a little too close. All of a sudden. I'm sorry, it was just a little too much like . . . another game I used to play. Don't look so concerned. It wasn't your fault."

"I won't try it again."

"That's probably better."

The coffee came. The silence was laborious. As we were

getting ready to leave, she suddenly gave me a strained and vivid smile and reached a trembling hand across to touch my wrist and said, "Darling, did you remember to mail the cards to Mom and Sis?"

"I mailed them. Your mother got the one of the bucks with their horns locked."

She pursed her lips for a moment, and I knew she was thinking how to cue me so I could win. "I wonder if Mom will think there's some kind of symbolism there, dear, and get upset or anything."

"Baby, fighting over dough is the thing she does best."

She laughed. Acknowledgment of defeat. Bad jokes win. Her eyes glistened, but she laughed. I was proud of her for coming through, but I could not help feeling guilty too. She had her adjustment, her acceptance. It wasn't fair to stir her up. It wasn't fair to her for me to want to see her lift a bit, to see what she looked like behind the iron control. Two games had set a pattern. We were Myra and Frank. If I tried another round, she would feel obligated. So I would leave it up to her to start the next one. And she would know I was leaving it up to her and why. That was the funny thing about us, back in the beginning. I had the absolute confidence in her knowing what I was thinking.

We went north up Route 8 into the hills. We went through a village named Poland. It looked like a Christmas card. The roads were dry, the snow banked high. It was the sort of town that you do not particularly want to live in, but wish you had come from. It looked like a very good place to be from.

Further up into the Adirondack Forest Preserve, the air was clearer and colder. The heater in the little sedan was comforting. Winding road, winter lakes, blackness of the evergreens against snow, tree-stubbled hills like the hump backs of old browsing beasts, eating away at eternity. At least we had changed the quality of our silences. Or that lovely land had changed it.

Speculator, at almost four in the afternoon, was about the size of Poland, but with about one-fifth the charm. Progress had begun to clomp down its main drag, whanging at a tin drum, sending off little clusters of neon. The ski kids were roaming the area, hooting their rut cries at each other, speckling the snow banks with their bright empty beer cans. I parked in front of a big supermarket-type general store called Chas Johns, where all the fluorescence was on in the gray dullness of the overcast afternoon, and Dana called from an outdoor phone booth. She was back in a few moments and said, "They say he went down to Gloversville to pick up a railway express shipment of skis or something, and they expect him back at six."

"So, accommodations I guess. I want a chance to measure him a little, get the right time and place to break him open."

"Remember, he'll recognize me."

"I know. And I may need you for the finale, after he's gone soft. We'll see."

"It's strange. You make him sound like a locked box."

"That's what they are, Dana. And usually somebody skimped on the design. Bad welds and a dime-store lock."

There was a small and relatively new motel jammed into almost the center of town at a strange angle. I made a try. The gentleman in command said he had one twin-bed room only because he had a cancellation, and he could let it go for one night only, because he was reserved from Thursday right through the weekend, and so was everybody else. It was good snow and a good forecast, and it looked like one of the big weeks of the season.

I went back out and got in behind the wheel and said, "Dana, I can't help how this sounds, believe me. It's a high-school routine all the way. You can go in and ask him." I told her what I'd learned, and said, "Suppose I take it and you drive back down to Utica and stay there and come on back out in the morning."

She hesitated for four seconds and then said, "If you'd just do something about that horrible snoring, see a doctor, anything, then we wouldn't have to go through this all the time."

"Myra, I freely admit I do breathe a little heavy."

"A little heavy! When you get going, the neighbors run out into the night screaming 'Lion, Lion'."

"Only when I get over onto my back, dear."

"Then you have a back on both sides. Anyway, dear, I'll sleep so well in this mountain air, I don't think you'll bother me tonight. But do try to hold it down to a dull roar."

"You act as if I enjoyed it."

"Because, my pet, you *sound* as if you were enjoying it."

A car came in and I was afraid we would lose the room if we waited the game out, so I went in and signed us in as T.

McGee and wife. The two three-quarter beds seemed to crowd the room. We did a lot of polite walking around each other, getting organized. An electric wall heater kept the room reasonably comfortable. With one quick trip to the ice machine, and with a considerable magic, she materialized a squat broad silver cup, the right amount of gin on ice, the two drops of bitters.

"The celebrity treatment?" I said ungraciously.

"I wouldn't want to get out of practice."

"Well . . . thanks. It's fine."

"You are so welcome, Travis."

We decided it would be best to leave her right there while I took the first little prod at Carl Abelle. The Mohawk Lodge was seven or eight miles out Indian Lake Road, over some impressively hilly highway. The grounds were aglare with floodlights against snow. The establishment was garishly new, pale varnished pine, A-frames, Swiss-kwaint gables. The sign advertised three tows, eight downhill runs, instruction, beginners' slope, Icelandic bathhouse, prime steaks, cocktails. The whole place was noisy, bursting at the seams, with much coming and going and giggling and hooting.

I worked my way into what seemed to be the main lounge. An ox could have been roasted on a spit in the fieldstone fireplace. The ceiling was low, beams huge. There were a lot of overstuffed couches and chairs, and deep rugs underfoot. There seemed to be a great number of young people sprawled on the floor. I saw several legs in casts, arms in slings. Sweating waiters brought drinks from a corner bar, stepping over and around the people, grimly ignoring the shouts for service. A big stereo juke made loud Beatle-music, and some snow bunnies were energetically trying to revive the Twist, wearing their indoor-fireside-snuggle-pants rather than their outdoor togs.

I angled toward a waiter and stuffed a bill in his shirt pocket. It bought me four seconds of attention. "Carl Abelle," I asked.

He pointed with his head, and said, "Red jacket."

Abelle was leaning against a paneled wall. He wore a red blazer with an Olympic pocket patch, silver buttons, a white silk ascot. He stood with his head bowed, a dainty little snow bunny in each arm. One of them was talking directly into his ear. She writhed and she worked her face in the curious manner of many women telling a dirty joke. I held off until she had made her point. Silvery glissandos from the girls. A hohoho from Abelle. I moved in and the three of them looked up at me with the polite glaze the in-groupers give the outsider. I wasn't wearing the garments.

The girls looked very young, and the out-of-doors had given them both a lovely healthy flush. But their eyes looked wise and old. Carl looked magnificent. The bronzed blond hero, white of tooth, clear of eye. But somehow it all looked like makeup. And in spite of the tailoring, he seemed to be getting a little thick around the middle.

"Abelle?"

"Yesss?"

"I bring you a message from friends."

"Zo?"

"From Cass. From Vance and Patty. From Lee and Sonny and Whippy and Nancy and the whole gang."

"I know zose people?"

"Yes, you know zose people." I didn't say any more. I let him hang there. He added them up. He wasn't very good at it. His face got sulky and wary.

"Oho," he said. "Would you mean Miss Abbott? And the M'Gruders?"

"And the Cornell boys too."

"Giff them all my best regards, ya?"

"That wasn't exactly the message, Carl."

"Zo?"

"If we could take a two-minute walk."

He hugged the bunnies, whispered to them, sent them off toward the fireplace with an identical little stroke at each upholstered little behind.

"Now we can talk here, Mister . . . .?"

"It's something in the car I want to show you."

"Bring it in."

"I'm sorry. I have to follow Miss Dean's instructions."

He gained a little confidence. "Zo, you work for her. A very lovely little lady, ya?"

"She sends her very special regards."

He puffed up very nicely. But then he remembered the names I had given him. He was not intellectualizing anything. He merely had the animal's awareness of something not quite right. "What could that dear woman send me you could not bring in?"

I winked at him most solemnly. "Herself."

He puffed up and he glowed. "Of courze!" He nudged me. "I understand."

"She isn't exactly waiting out in the car, you understand. She's at a private lodge down by the lake. She heard you were here. She said it was a very pleasant surprise. She's staying with old friends. Incognito."

"She sent you to bring me there?"

"On impulse. You understand."

"Oh, of courze!"

"Shall we go?"

He nibbled at his mouth, an Airedale frown between the hero brows. "I must come back later. Social obligations here. But yes, it would be rude not to come at once."

We went out to the rental car. His red blazer was handsome in the floodlights, between the snow banks. He strutted. There was a Teutonic wrinkle across the back of his neck. Maybe it had grown there in response to the faked accent. I had two inches in height, and he had at least fifteen pounds in weight. I couldn't risk taking any sporting chance with him. He might know how.

I hurried past him and opened the car door for him. He accepted it with regal satisfaction. As he started to bend to duck into the car, I screwed my feet firmly into the packed snow, pivoted very smartly, and with the best right hook I have, made a very good attempt to drive that middle silver button of the jacket right through to his backbone. These little melodramas always make me feel like a jackass. But you must do them briskly. A sudden, merciless, ugly violence is the great leveler. Men revert to childhood. The night is full of spooks and ghosties, and they are reminded of death. A man whipped in a fair fight retains stubborn remnants of pride and honor. A man rendered helpless without warning is much more suggestible. With a great gassy belch, he doubled. With hands clasped together, I chopped down against the back of his neck, off to one side, just below the mastoid bone. As he crumpled, I body-blocked him into the car, kicked his dangling legs inside and slammed the door. I imagine it took about three and a half seconds.

I got behind the wheel. He was edged partially under the dash. His relaxation was total. I could hear him snore. A few hundred yards down the highway I pulled over, hauled him onto the seat, removed his white silk scarf and tied his wrists together with it. I tied them together in crossed position, under his husky thighs. He toppled over against the door and moaned. Pathos in silver buttons. The world is shiny and the surface is a little too frangible. Something can reach out of the black and grab you at any moment. Everybody wears a different set of compulsions. You can be maimed without warning, in body or in spirit, by a very nice guy. It is the luck of your draw. I did not feel like a nice guy. His red coat was a little too brave and pretty. Now it was a child's toy on the beach after the child drowns. This one was not villainous. He was just a silly stud. A ski-slope, and less reptilian, version of Harry Diadem, a specialist in racing wax and erogenous zones.

I drove on down into Speculator, looking for a place to take him. The snow banks made it difficult. I turned west on Route 8, and after about a mile I found a darkened structure on the right, some sort of a building supply establishment. The drive and parking lot in the rear had been plowed out. Nearby houses were dark. I could see no pedestrians in the glow of the spaced street lights of the village. No traffic was coming in either direction at the moment. So I turned in quickly, skidding the back end, bumping it off a snow bank, turning off the car lights as I reached the parking lot. I backed it around behind the building, ready to head out. I got out quickly, looking around to see if I had attracted any attention. Snow laid a silence across the land. A dog barked, a comfortable distance away. Night sky speckled with silver. Bare trees in silhouette. Moving flicker of light as cars went by. It was about twenty degrees, I guessed, not too uncomfortable with no wind.

I opened the door on his side. He was coming out of it enough to strain for balance, but he came rolling out, onto the packed soiled snow of the parking area. I bent, braced myself well, and picked him up, the two hundred and twenty or so pounds of him, striving to make it seem effortless. The mature male is seldom picked up. It resonates the lost memories of babyhood. It induces a feeling of helplessness. I walked four strides with him, and dropped him into the slope of the five-foot bank of bulldozed snow, dropped him butt first, as into an armchair. He chunked down into it, tilted slightly back, feet free, knees up, lashed wrists holding him hunched and about as helpless as a man can be.

He shook his splendid leonine head slowly and said, "Sick. Real sick. Please."

When anything begins to fit their television or movie preconceptions they try to move toward the hero role. So one must give it a flavor they can't comprehend. Cops are good at it. Jocular. You can learn a lot from cop technique.

I stood close and reached to him and rumpled his blond locks with the casual affection you extend toward a small boy. I chuckled. I patted his cheek three times, and on the fourth pat I gave it a little more steam. It was not a blow, yet not a pat. It was a sharp demand for attention. Pay attention to teacher, boy.

My eyes had adjusted. I could see him clearly. Things had moved too quickly for him. He was staring at me with a dumb willingness to ingratiate himself. It was exactly the right attitude. It was a cheap tin box and a joke lock, and it had opened at a touch.

"Carl, baby, Lee is over a thousand miles from here, and she wouldn't say hello if she met you on the street."

"What are you . . ."

"She's a big investment. The people I work for get very nervous about her. You can understand that, Carl baby."

"I don't know what you . . ."

"They are very very annoyed with you, sweetie. You've been very stupid and very naughty. And you've gotten their investment very upset. You shouldn't have played ball with the people who wanted to give Lee a hard time. You should have realized we'd come after you sooner or later, baby."

"This is some kind of a mis . . ."

"Don't play dumb. It's too late for that. You have had it. They don't give me much discretion. At the very least, Carl, I have to break you up a little. Like two or three weeks' worth. And at the very most, I get my little shovel out of the truck and stick you under this snow."

The bulge of his eyes tipped me, so when the mouth opened wide for a roar of terror and protest, I packed it swiftly with a handful of snow. After he had coughed and huffed and spat, I used a handkerchief to wipe the snow water off his face. His teeth clittered. He was melting himself wet, but it was fright and cold both.

"Please!" he said. "I don't know what . . ."

I rumpled his hair again. "The *pictures,* sweetie! The

photographs, the pics, the way she got set up for it on that terrace. Like this one."

I had it in an inside pocket, folded once. I held it in front of his eyes, a lighter flame off to one side. A Lysa Dean sandwich. I put it away when he closed his eyes.

"Oh," he said weakly. "Oh God."

I said softly, "Now can you tell me a *good* reason why you shouldn't die young, sweetie?"

seven

I GOT BACK to the motel room a few minutes before nine. The door was unlocked. As I came in, Dana got up from the room's only armchair and came toward me, silhouetted against the lamp light.

"You were gone so long," she said.

The room was warm. I took my jacket off and stretched out on one of the beds. "A long time and a long way away," I said. "Scratch one ski instructor. We can leave now, if you want."

She looked down at me for a few moments, and then went and fixed another drink in that silver cup. I perched on one elbow and sipped it. "A lot bigger than the last one," I said.

"It seemed like a good idea."

"You've got good instincts." She sat on the foot of the bed. I shifted my feet to make room for her.

"Did . . . you hurt him?"

"I didn't leave a mark on him. I just finished sneaking him to his room up there at the lodge. He didn't want anybody to see him. His legs didn't work very well. I had to help him out of the car. I had to walk him, with my arm around his waist. He was crying like a kid. He had the snuffles. He kept telling me how grateful he was I didn't kill him. He likes me. It's a quick dependency relationship, something like getting emotionally hooked on your psychiatrist. At his door I patted him on the shoulder and told him to get a good night's rest. No, Dana, I didn't leave any visible marks. But I left the other kind. They last longer."

After a silence she said, "Trav, why do you do this sort of thing if it bothers you so much?"

"Maybe I like it. Maybe that's what bothers me."

"Look at me and tell me you like it."

"Okay. So it was just smart-ass talk. I left him with less. Less assurance, less faith, less confidence. Maybe his mask will start to slip a little from now on. The tone of voice won't be exactly right. The snow bunnies will detect it. And one of them will be a little too knowing, and push the right buttons, and big Carl Abelle will come up impotent just once. Once is all it will take, because that's about all he's got left."

She put her hand on my ankle, a light quick touch, like a pat of assurance. "Travis, if you can feel this way, and keep on feeling this way, isn't it all right for you? What if you should become indifferent to . . . this business of opening people up like little dirty boxes?"

"Maybe I care less now than I did a few years back."

"Is Abelle so valuable?"

"Isn't that the key to it, Dana? This act of judging the value of anyone? Is it something I am entitled to do for money? If we're judging value, why am I working for your boss?"

"Why am I?" We watched each other. Suddenly she grinned. "Don't try to fool me or yourself, McGee. If you'd learned anything important from him, you wouldn't be acting like this."

I admitted it. She fixed me a new drink. I told her what I had learned. Not very much. He was certain of one thing. No one had followed Lysa Dean to the Chipmann house. None of the playmates could have tipped anybody off that she was there, because he had not said who he was shacked with, and after they all got there, no one left until it was all over, and the phone was disconnected. Cass was Caswell Edgars, a San Francisco artist. Abelle had not known that Nancy Abbott had gone off with Sonny Catton, nor that Sonny was dead. He had confirmed that Nancy had been houseguesting with the M'Gruders in Carmel, and had said that Vance M'Gruder was a friend of Alex Abbott, Nancy's elder brother.

"Nothing else?" she asked.

"Just guesses. But how good are they? A terrorized man tries to please, like a hypnotic subject. Rule out the Cornell boys. Rule out Cass Edgars and the waitress. And, according to Abelle, we can rule out Lysa Dean too. Security was good. So who was the target? Nancy Abbott? Vance M'Gruder? Patty M'Gruder? There's money there. Blackmail targets. Miss Dean was pure profit. The pictures sent Nancy's father were not the same as the ones sent Lee. Okay, so the fellow took perhaps a dozen rolls. Two dozen. Two hundred and fifty to five hundred shots. He could have another set to sell Vance, another to sell Patty, maybe a set for everybody until he could find out which ones had the money. Maybe he started out, for God's sake, after nesting water birds and hit a jackpot on the terrace a hundred yards away."

"But the idea of it being an accident doesn't appeal?"

"No. Before they bought the groceries, they all knew the name of the absentee owners of the house where they were going. If it was set up, either somebody in the group, during the milling around before they took off in the cars, tipped the cameraman off. Or they were being followed. Somehow I like the first choice, Dana. It goes with the way the party developed, as if it was being staged that way."

"Could he tell you who started it?"

"He said it just happened. Everybody tight. One of those real swinging parlor games, revised for a sun terrace. Somebody gets blindfolded, crawls around, and the first person they touch has to hold still, not make a sound, and be identified by touch. Guess right and the one identified loses one item they're wearing, and gets the blindfold. Guess wrong and the guesser loses one item and tries again."

"Sounds gaudy."

"He said nobody really started it. They made up the rules as they went along."

"With much jolly laughter."

"It's a funny thing about Abelle. He had absolutely no idea any pictures were taken. But he did have the feeling that something was wrong. And he is not a sensitive guy. He couldn't put it into words. After the group had broken up and he was alone again with Lee, he had the feeling that something was going to work out badly for somebody."

"Wouldn't anyone have that feeling after all that?"

"If it was new to them, I guess so. But Abelle has had that kind of group action before and since, and the other times didn't hit him that way. *Something* gave him that feeling.

Somebody made him react that way. But he was drunk. I couldn't dig it out. He had the feeling somebody was going to kill somebody sooner or later, because of that house party."

"Where do we go next, Travis?"

"I want to know how Nancy Abbott's father got her pictures, and if there was any more contact."

I put the silver cup aside. It seemed that moments later Dana was gently shaking me awake. There was a delicious aroma in the room. She had walked to a place almost next door called The Log Cabin Restaurant, eaten there and brought me back a huge bowl of homemade clam chowder and a broiled hamburger as thick as her wrist. It tasted as fine as it smelled.

I awoke again. The room was dark. My shoes were off. There was a blanket over me, but the cold had awakened me. A glow of the sign outside came through the blinds, and I could see the sleeping shape of her in the other bed, hair dark against the pillow. I made a silent trip to the bathroom, came back and undressed to my shorts and slipped into the cool sheets and was asleep in an instant. You can seldom guess what will exhaust you emotionally. That hulk of brave muscle had been a weak and pretentious child. In my dreams I heard him sob. Oh please don't. Oh please. Oh please, mister.

She had flight schedules indicating we could do better out of Syracuse. So we got an early start and went down to the Thruway and west to the Syracuse airport, through a cold gray morning and some tentative snow flurries. She found the best way out, through to Chicago and then non-stop to San Francisco. I noticed something about her, in the ticketing and the baggage arrangements and turning in the rental car, and even with the stewardesses. With absolutely no fuss at all, she got the maximum service merely by an attitude— smiling and polite—which seemed to make anything less than perfect service unthinkable. She could raise one eyebrow and bring a porter hustling from eighty feet away. It is a rare gift. I tried to take over some of the chores, but it seemed to make her feel uncomfortable. It was her job and she was used to it, and she knew how to keep everything straight. I had all the benefit of her efficiency. People stared at me as though trying to remember where they had seen me. This knack of getting exactly what you want exactly when you want it is something shared by great ladies, royalty and the very best executive secretaries. Also I must admit that her strong and handsome face, and the sparkling intensity of her dark eyes gave the impression that if things did not go her way, all hell would break loose immediately. But it was odd to have someone else taking such efficient care. I began to feel a little like the honeymoon bride of an important widower. Or a boy being taken to camp by one of those super-mothers.

She tried to resist being given a window seat. After we'd latched the seat belts, she checked her little note book and said, "We'll have an hour and fifty minutes in Chicago. I'll make some phone calls from there. Are you perfectly comfortable, Travis? Is there anything you'd like?"

"You'd better hustle up forward and help them with the check list for takeoff, honey."

Her mouth tightened and her face got slightly red. "I'm not trying to be officious."

"You are a little overwhelming, Dana."

"You could do it all just as well. But why should you?"

"Okay. Thanks. You're very good."

It was not gracious. Most of my women have not been particularly useful outside the home. I looked at her emotionless profile and sighed and said, "Aw come *on*, Myra."

Reluctantly her mouth softened. "You get these ugly moods, Frank."

"I keep worrying about how things are going back at the office."

"Honey, I bet they hardly know you're gone."

"Oh, thanks. Thanks a lot. That's a big help." She was laughing with me. Her eyes laughed too. It went deep. That kind of affection is seriously underrated among the hack and grab set. To whom should they give trust? To someone who likes them. When she laughed or smiled broadly I could see that one of the eyeteeth, the one on the left, was set in there aslant, making a little overlap with the tooth in front of it. When an imperfection looks very dear to you, heed the message. Lysa Dean's teeth were mercilessly perfect. No message there. Maybe some of my awareness made a little mark. Dana Holtzer suddenly stopped the real laughter, and went along for a little while on some fake laughter, and then folded herself back into herself, out of sight and out of reach, becoming once again the secretarial presence beside me, smart in wool, laced, girdled, hammocked and erect, her neck severe, eyes distant, seat belt pulled tight for takeoff.

Alexander Armitage Abbott, A.I.A., lay dying in room 310 of University Hospital in San Francisco. There was a waiting room at the end of the corridor. A gray rain which was going to continue forever streaked the waiting room windows, obscuring the view of gray hills. It was Friday afternoon. Dana and I sat like dulled passengers in a heavy train sidetracked at the end of noplace. She put a frayed magazine back in the rack and came over to sit beside me on the couch.

"You're doing finc," I told her.

"I don't like that young man. Or his wife."

"It shows a little. It doesn't hurt anything. They're not anxious to be liked."

The young man came back. Not as young as he looked, or perhaps tried to look. Nancy's brother. Alex. Meaty, dark, bland. The kind who have a smell of pine and a perfect manicure. He gave us a smile of measured sadness and sat facing us. "Sorry about the constant interruptions. You know how it is." He shrugged. "One or the other of us should be with him. It seems to help him a little. Elaine is being so good about it. You have no idea."

"I guess he wouldn't want to see Nancy," Dana said innocently.

"God, no!" Alex said. "I believe, I really believe that he might have lived years longer if it wasn't . . . for all the shame and heartbreak she's given him. She's my only sister. But I can't be the least bit sentimental. Some people are just born rotten." He made a helpless gesture. "Nothing we've tried to do for her has done any good. She's made life difficult . . . for all of us."

"You understand our viewpoint in this, Mr. Abbott," I said.

"Of course. Of course. I appreciate the fact you want to handle this on a completely informal basis. I think I understand her present condition, as well as Mr. Burley's concern. And I am perfectly willing to write to him personally guaranteeing the thousand dollars a month for as long as . . . as she can remain there. Frankly, I was responsible for the selection of the retreat. I wanted her just as far from San Francisco as possible. Dad is leaving her nothing, of course. But I can tell you in confidence that the estate is . . . sizable.

And I would consider it a moral obligation. I'm very glad you and Miss Holtzer had to come here on another matter. It's good to talk this over."

I sensed that he was trying to brush us off. Thanks and goodby. He was an elusive fellow. "We haven't settled it yet, Mr. Abbott," I told him. "Mr. Burley has certain moral obligations too, and he is aware of them. He is not set up to give her the mental care she needs. Under the present arrangement, he can't afford to bring someone there at regular intervals to treat her there. We are functioning here merely as . . . friends of Hope Island, Mr. Abbott."

"I understand, but . . ."

"If the monthly fee could be doubled . . ."

"That's out of the question," he said with a regretful air. "I guess it would be better if Mr. Burley did arrange commitment to a mental institution, if that's what he thinks she needs."

"There's just one small problem," I said. "At times she seems perfectly healthy and rational. And she has built up a whole structure of conspiracy. We understand that it isn't true, of course, but it does sound very plausible, and if she went to some other place, they might think it necessary to make a complete investigation."

"I don't believe I understand," he said.

I glanced at Dana and nodded and she took over. "Nancy insists that a year and a half ago, you put her in the custody of some people in Carmel named M'Gruder."

"In the custody!" he said indignantly. "It wasn't like that at all. They were just helping me out. They knew Nancy, of course. They knew she could be a problem. It was just a case of getting her away from a very unsavory group she was running with, and . . ."

"I am just telling you Nancy's story. We all know she isn't well, Mr. Abbott. She claims that the M'Gruders, as a favor to you, got her drunk and got her into a situation where certain pictures were taken of her under compromising circumstances. These pictures were then sent to your father so you could be certain you would be the sole heir. She claims you and your father then tried to put her away, but she fled and remained at large for quite a while until you caught up to her and sent her to Hope Island."

Dana did beautifully with it. I watched his face. He had a big choice of reactions. He tried for amused indignation, and almost made it. But not quite. You have to watch for the not-quites.

"Do you mean to tell me she could make anyone believe such nonsense?"

"Not necessarily," I said. "They might want to check it out."

"But why?"

I nodded to Dana. She took the picture from her big purse. I slipped it out of the envelope and leaned and handed it to Alex Abbott. He held it in two trembling hands and stared at it. He swallowed convulsively. In a small voice he said, "This one wasn't . . ." He caught himself. "She had this? My sister had this?"

"This is one of several. Mr. Burley has them in his safe."

"But where would she get them? She didn't have them when she was taken down there?"

"They came to her in the mail," I said. "Mr. Abbott, what was it you started to say? This one wasn't . . . This one wasn't what?"

He opened his eyes very wide. He smiled sadly. "I guess I should be frank with you people."

"We would be most grateful," Dana said.

"I will admit that I made a mistake when I . . . arranged her visit with the M'Gruders. I knew them as a lively couple. I thought they would keep her amused and out of trouble. I had no idea they went in for this sort of thing." He handed it back to me.

"I would think you would act a little more angry," I said,

"To tell you the truth, there were other pictures of Nancy. They were mailed to my father, with a note demanding money. He had a very nasty scene with Nancy. She left. He showed me the pictures. He was wretched. Heartbroken. He asked me to destroy the pictures and I did so, very gladly. Several days later, after Nancy was gone, someone phoned my father about the money. He told them to go to hell, that they could do any damn thing with the pictures they pleased."

"He didn't contact the police?"

"No."

"Did the man on the phone threaten him with anything?"

"No. Dad said the man was quite polite. He seemed to have some sort of lower-class English accent. He said he might phone back later on, but as far as I know he never did.

In one of the pictures it was . . . well, it was Vance M'Gruder and my sister. I can tell you that I was furious with him. I went down to see him. He was alone at the house. Patty had left him. I learned later their marriage was being annulled. He didn't seem guilty or ashamed or anything like that. Just terribly indifferent. I couldn't make a dent on him. He said he was not and had never been in the nursemaid business, no matter what impression I may have had. He did not know or care where Nancy was. I actually thought I might find her there with them. I wanted to know who had taken the pictures at that . . . circus."

"Did he know?"

"He said that nobody at the party had taken them. He said it had to be someone with a long lens."

"Did he seem surprised to know pictures had been taken?"

"No. I wondered if he'd been approached for money also."

"Did you ask him?"

"No. He seemed cross and impatient and anxious for me to go."

"Did you know any of the other people in the pictures you saw?"

"Aside from the M'Gruders, just one fellow, an artist I . . ." He stopped suddenly, frowning at us. "Why are you so curious about the pictures, Mr. McGee?"

I shrugged. "I guess it's only natural. Mr. Burley was curious too. They do have some bearing on the girl's evaluation of herself. I suppose if she feels it was a conspiracy, a trick, she feels better about it."

"Mr. McGee, if Nancy ever had any hopes of inheriting half the estate, she spoiled her chances long before those pictures were taken, believe me. Naturally I'll support her as long as she lives. But what you ask seems . . ."

"Oh, I don't think she could cause you much trouble, Mr. Abbott."

"I don't see how she could cause any."

I smiled and shrugged. "An institution might call in somebody to give her legal advice. You know how it is. Contingency basis. And you say the estate is sizable. She does sound plausible. All it could do, I guess, would be delay the probate."

He studied his thumbnail. He bit a small piece out of the corner of it and got up and went to the steel window and teetered back and forth, heel to toe.

"You say she seems happy there at the Island?"

"She has friends there. And the illusion of freedom."

Without turning, he said, "And this deterioration you mention. It is progressive?"

"From all indications."

"I imagine that if I footed the bill for additional care for . . . say another six months, by the end of that time she . . ."

"Let's say eighteen months."

"I'll take my chances on a year. No more."

"I will so inform Mr. Burley."

He looked at his watch. "Elaine gets nervous if I leave her in there too long. Uh . . . thanks for the report. Goodby." He walked out without looking directly at either of us.

On the way down in the elevator, Dana looked at me and slowly shook her head. "You are very damn good, Trav. You are better than I realized. You are shameless. You are a bastard, Trav. You know very damn well he thinks you are going to split the increase with Mr. Burley. He thinks you are going to bring suit in her name if he doesn't play. And you sat there, so righteous and kindly. Oh boy, oh boy."

"A man like that can't believe anything that doesn't sound crooked."

"A man like that makes me want to go scrub. They better not leave him alone with dear Dad. He's impatient."

Before I started the car I turned to her and said, "Itemize."

"What? Oh. He didn't have the pictures taken. The man who took them or had them taken has a cheap British accent. M'Gruder knew about the pictures. And something else. Let me think. Oh, the M'Gruder marriage was annulled. Did I miss anything?"

"You are very good too."

"I am afflicted with an orderly mind."

And so we drove back to the heart of the city. San Francisco is the most depressing city in America. The come-latelys might not think so. They may be enchanted by the steep streets up Nob and Russian and Telegraph, by the sea mystery of the Bridge over to redwood country on a foggy night, by the urban compartmentalization of Chinese, Spanish, Greek, Japanese, by the smartness of the women and the city's iron clutch on culture. It might look just fine to the new ones.

But there are too many of us who used to love her. She was like a wild classy kook of a gal, one of those rain-walkers, laughing gray eyes, tousle of dark hair—sea misty, a lithe and lively lady, who could laugh at you or with you, and at herself when needs be. A sayer of strange and lovely things. A girl to be in love with, with love like a heady magic.

But she had lost it, boy. She used to give it away, and now she sells it to the tourists. She imitates herself. Her figure has thickened. The things she says now are mechanical and memorized. She overcharges for cynical services.

Maybe if you are from Dayton or Amarillo or Wheeling or Scranton or Camden she can look like magic to you because you have not had a chance to see what a city can be. This one had her chance to go straight and she lost it somehow, and it has been downhill for her ever since. That's why she is so depressing to those of us who knew her when. We all know what she could have been, and we all know the lousy choice she made. She has driven away the ones who loved her best. A few keep trying. Herb Caen. A few others. But the love words have a hollow tone these days.

eight

INVESTIGATING a cold cold trail can be deadly dull and very discouraging. This one worked pretty well, perhaps because there were two of us, two sets of hunches, two sets of ideas, two methods of approach.

We found Caswell Edgars in Sausalito. He looked twenty pounds heavier than in the pictures. He was living in a pig-pen litter in the expensive home of a skinny drift-wood blonde on the far side of fifty. She was there too, in extreme-ly tight pants and a high girlish giggle. Any minute now Cas-sie was going to start working hard getting ready for a one-man show she was going to arrange for him. They had a music system that would have blown the walls out of a less substantial structure. She had soiled ankles, a grubby neck, and a black eye which had faded to saffron. They were hooked on something. From the way they acted, I suspect one of the hypnotics. The house smelled like old laundry. There was a loose and dangerous and desperate flavor about the alliance, and it was easy to imagine that in their blundering they would sooner or later manage to set fire to the place and scream with laughter until they found all exits blocked. She kept talking about poor little ole Henry, who seemed to be a husband, but I could not determine if he was living or dead. If dead, it was conceivable he was buried in the yard, under the weeds. Edgars knew absolutely nothing about any pic-tures. But he had no difficulty remembering the occasion. He had musician talk which he didn't do too well. "Man, that was a bash. That little movie piece was pure stone fox. The

85

boss fox of all time. Somebody trying to scuffle her with the pics? You never said, man."

"No. I never said."

"Sonny traded the waitress for the tall brunette, and then he burned. It's a harsh way to make bread, man, that chance of burning. I read it someplace."

"Put on my records, Cassie doll baby bug, huh?"

I don't think either of them noticed we'd left, or cared particularly. Though it was warm in the car, Dana shuddered.

"Scratch one more contestant, Dana doll baby bug."

"Please don't," she said in a thin voice.

"Like they say, lives of quiet desperation."

"Trav?"

"Yes?"

"I think that terrace was a damned unlucky place to be. Sonny Catton, Nancy Abbott, Carl Abelle . . . and Caswell Edgars."

"Punishment from on high?"

"I don't know. Maybe. Maybe it can happen, Trav."

She took care of Carmel with some phone calls. The M'Gruder place had been sold almost a year ago. We had less luck with newspaper accounts. I did dig up some background on M'Gruder. There had been an elder brother, killed in a war. M'Gruder's father had invented a little gadget. Every cracking plant in the world had to have one or two of them. Vance M'Gruder had married one Patricia Gedley-Davies some three years ago in California, after apparently importing her from London. She had crewed for him in smaller sailboats. There was no social prominence, nor any attempt apparently to achieve any. But there was money, and so one would think the annulment would be more than a six-line paragraph on page 36. It had happened about two months after the house party.

Dana Holtzer sat in my hotel room with her shoes off and her feet up, frowning thoughtfully after having made a Sunday afternoon call to Lysa Dean.

"This annulment thing," she said. "What you think of, in a state with a community property law, it's the cheap way out."

"Yes indeed."

"And this was a closed session or closed hearing or whatever you call it, just the judge and them and a lawyer, and everybody agreeing to everything, and a declaration by the judge that the marriage had never existed in fact or something. And this wasn't a humble woman, Trav. Sort of noisy and bossy. Let's say she came from nothing, and she married a rich man. Would she give up without a battle? What made her give up without a battle?"

"And where is she?"

We couldn't answer our questions, but we could look for answers. I decided we would split up on Monday, to save time. I would pursue a small idea of my own. She would use Lloyd's Register as her guide book, and work the boaty people, the ocean sailing types, with appropriate cover story, and see what she could get in the way of gossip.

It rained all day, matching the mood of the offices I visited. Investigation agencies have very little need for decor. They like to keep the overhead down. Their usual customer does not shop around, looking for better draperies. Most of them are sad, soft, pale, meaty people. They operate with about the same verve as do the people who come to spray your home with bug juice.

I had my lines down pat by the time I hit the third one. My name was Jones, said with that emphasis which indicated it was anything but Jones. My employment was "managing my own investment program." That brought a little flicker into tired eyes. My young Italian wife was playing around. I was positive of two men. Perhaps there were three. I wanted somebody who could get some flagrante pictures of her, very quietly and inconspicuously, without her knowing. Then, with the pictures in hand, I could dicker with her and get out of the marriage without too much expense.

No sir, we don't do that kind of thing.

Who does? Where should I go?

I just wouldn't know, mister.

At four o'clock I hit one who was sufficiently unsavory and hungry. He had the cop look. Not the good cop look, but the apple-stealing look. It was a very good guess that he had been busted for the wrong combination of greed and stupidity, and that he wasn't going to do too well in this line of work either. He had a desk in one of those warehouse offices, the kind where you get the desk, the mail drop, switchboard service and an hourly rate on secretarial help—along with a ragtag collection of phone solicitors, speculators in distressed merchandise, independent jewelry salesmen and so on.

He listened to my story and looked at me with the concealed anguish of a toothless crocodile inspecting a fat brown dog on the river bank. He wanted to know how to get at me. We hitched chairs close and hunched toward each other. He had that breath which exceptionally bad teeth can create.

"Now, Mr. Jones, I maybe can help and maybe I can't. A thing like this, it would be strickly a cash arrangement. You unnerstand?"

"Of course."

"Now I've got a guy in mind. He's tops. What he goes after, he gets. But he comes high."

"How high?"

"Considering the risks and all I would say this guy couldn't be touched for less than five thousand, but he's a real pro, and he will come up with shots of that little two-timing wop that'll nail her but good. This guy, he's got all the techniques and equipment, but he's funny. He doesn't feel like working, he doesn't work."

"I never heard of such a thing."

"Like an artist, like, he's got temperamental, you know?"

"I guess I know what you mean."

"What would happen, he would work through me. Now I don't want to be wasting my time trying to talk him into anything. What I need, I need a guarantee of good faith on your part, I mean that you want to go ahead at least far enough to take care of the first part of the trouble I'm going to, namely trying to get him on the phone long distance."

I took my wallet out below the desk edge, took a hundred-dollar bill and put it near his elbow. "Is this okay?"

A big paw fell on it and it was gone. With the back of the other paw he wiped his mouth. "Just fine. Now you go wait out in the hall. There's a bench out there to sit on."

I sat for nearly fifteen minutes. Odd-looking people came and went, tenants and clients and customers. Underside people. The ones that somehow seem to be clinging to the damp underside of reality. The ones that look as if they could truly astonish a psychiatrist or a bacteriologist.

He came out and hunkered in close beside me, to rot my collar with his foul exhalations. "What happened, I can't get him, but the way it looks I got some leads, there's somebody can do a nice job, give me a little time on it."

"Why can't you get the man you were talking about?"

"He's been dead a while. I didn't know that. I didn't hear about it, the way things are, him out of town."

"What was his name?"

"There are guys around just as good. What I want, you give me how I can get in touch with you, and when I get a good man lined up, one I can guarantee will do this little job, then . . ."

"I'll give you a ring in a few days."

"On account of I got to do some digging to find the exact right guy for your problem, what about you give me the same figure again as a retainer?"

"We better talk about that if you can find anybody."

After a few more half-hearted attempts, he went shuffling back into his rental bull pen, pants droopy in the seat, hair grizzled gray on the nape of his thick neck.

I made it to the nearest rancid saloon in about eight big bounds, shut myself into a phone booth and called back. I had remembered the name of the switchboard girl on duty. It was posted on her board.

"Miss Ganz, this is Sergeant Zimmerman. Bunco Squad. Within the past twenty minutes you placed a long distance call for Gannon."

"Who? What?"

"Please give me the name, number and location of the call he placed."

"But I'm not supposed to . . ."

"I can send for you, Miss Ganz, and have you brought down here if you want it that way."

"Did . . . did you say Zimmerman?"

"If you want to play it safe, Miss Ganz, call me back here at headquarters. We have a separate number." I gave her the pay phone number. She had been starting to cool off, and I had to take the chance or get nothing.

In thirty seconds the phone rang. I put my thumb in the side of my mouth, raised my tone level a half octave and said, "Bunco, Halpern."

"Sergeant Zimmerman, please."

"Just a minute." After a ten count, I said, "Zimmerman."

"This is Miss Ganz," she said briskly. "About what you wanted, the call was to a Mr. D. C. Ives, in Santa Rosita.

805-765-4434. That number had been disconnected. Then he called a Mr. Mendez in Santa Rosita, 805-384-7942. They talked for less than three minutes. Is that what you wanted, Sergeant?"

"Thank you very much for your cooperation, Miss Ganz. We'll protect our source in this matter. We may have to ask you for some other favor along the same line in the future."

"You're very welcome," she said.

A nice efficient careful girl. She had to make certain she was really talking to the cops.

Dana got back to the hotel a little after six. She looked pallid and twitchy. Her smile came and went too quickly. She had called me as soon as she got in, and I went down the hallway to her room. A woman in that condition needs to be hugged and held and patted a little. But we weren't on any kind of basis where I could do that.

I lit her trembling cigarette and then she switched around the room and said, "I am now a real drinking buddy of Mrs. T. Madison Devlaney III. I call her Squeakie, as does practically everyone. I poured drinks into her potted plants. Until she passed out. She is twenty-nine. She is two days younger than Vance M'Gruder. She has known him all her life. She has a teeny little voice, ten thousand freckles, ten million dollars, and she's muscled like a circus girl. Swimming every morning, tennis every afternoon, potted every night. No tennis today. Strained ankle."

"What cover story did she buy?"

"Trav, don't be angry, but I couldn't have gotten to her at all without using the best connection I have. Lysa Dean. That opens a lot of doors. And I do have those calling cards."

"I didn't say you shouldn't. I just said don't use her if you don't have to."

"I had to. I told her that Lysa had met Vance. I told her that Lysa was forming a little production company of her own and, as a first picture, was thinking of basing it on one of the ocean races, perhaps the race to Hawaii, and she was asking me to find out just how much cooperation she could get from the people who do own the big boats. It's nonsense, of course, but people know so little about the industry they're ready to believe anything. I made up sort of a plot as I went along."

"So she bought it. That's the important thing. What about M'Gruder?"

"Let me see. Oh, lots of things about M'Gruder. He is a physical fitness nut. He is a fine deep-water sailor. He is fantastically stingy. He gets quarrelsome and violent when he gets drunk. The marriage to Patricia Gedley-Davies was, according to his friends, a grotesque mistake. She said that forty-two times at least. Grotesque mistake. Squeakie and her friends are convinced Patty was a London call girl. I wouldn't say that anyone is particularly fond of Vance, but they are glad to see that marriage ended. They think it was bad form. And so lucky there were no children." She took out her little note book. "The new wife is supposed to be enchanting. Her name is Ulka Atlund. She turned eighteen a few days before their marriage. Her mother is dead. Her father brought her over here two years ago. He came to lecture for a year at the University of San Francisco, and stayed for a second year. He opposed the marriage, then agreed on the basis that after the honeymoon, she continues her education. They plan to honeymoon for six months. They've been gone two months. Squeakie thinks she heard somewhere that Vance plans to have somebody else bring the boat back from Acapulco. Too much beating into the wind on the way back. She thinks Vance planned to spend that last two months of the honeymoon in his house at Hawaii. Then back to live here while Ulka goes back to college."

"What about the annulment?"

"This is where it gets pretty untidy, Travis."

I got tired of the way she was roving around. I got her wrists and pushed her gently back until the backs of her legs hit the edge of a chair. She sat down and looked up at me, startled.

"Let me tell you something, Miss Holtzer. This whole deal is untidy. The stupendous glamor of Lysa Dean did not suck me into this. You were the item that swayed me."

"What? What?"

"If she'd sent anyone else, the answer would have been no. You looked so staunch and loyal and unyielding and severe. So damned *decent*. You made me feel like an unwashed opportunist. I have emotional reactions to people, Dana, no matter how much I try to deny it. I wanted to prove to you that I am good at what I do."

"But that's absurd!"

I backed away and sat on her bed. "It certainly is. Now, how untidy does this situation get?"

She shrugged. "Squeakie doesn't know for sure. Just second-hand and third-hand gossip. But Nancy Abbott came into it. Apparently, among Squeakie's set, the favorite theory is that Patty M'Gruder had Nancy as a house guest in Carmel, and practically held her a prisoner there, because she . . . Patty . . . had fallen in love with Nancy. The theory is that Vance went along with it because it gave him a chance to get the proof he wanted that Patty had entered into the marriage contract under false pretenses, concealing her real inclinations. Vance used Nancy. . . . Squeakie kept calling her 'that poor poor sick child' . . . to get the proof, and once he had it, there was no way in the world for Patty to fight his action to annul. It was all handled very quietly."

"That would explain what Nancy yelled at me, about Patty keeping her locked up."

"I suppose so. Patty left. Squeakie's phrase for it was that she slunk away. Somebody saw her several weeks ago, in Las Vegas. Not in one of the big places out on the Strip. Down in town, working at something called The Four Treys. Making change, I think. Some kind of a small job. There certainly wouldn't be many old friends seeing her there. Anyway, Mrs. T. Madison Devlaney didn't know anything about . . . or at least say anything about any pictures. I was lucky to catch her. She and her husband and another couple are flying to Hawaii this week. That whole group seems to be very big for Hawaii. The Devlaneys keep a boat out there."

"You did very well, Dana."

"Thank you. They have a beautiful home. She really got terribly drunk. Did you learn anything at all?"

"I don't know. I traced a man who could have taken the pictures. But he lived three hundred miles away. It looks as if M'Gruder had the pictures taken. I think we can assume that, at least for now. But I can't prove any contact between M'Gruder and the photographer. One thing makes me think I located the right man. He's dead."

"I beg your pardon?"

"Let's say that just for kicks or souvenirs or something he kept one set of prints for himself. He died. Those files got into the hands of somebody who . . ."

"Of course."

"His name was D. C. Ives, possibly. And he lived in Santa Rosita, possibly. We check him out for a vulgar limey accent, and if so it will look a lot more certain."

"Is that what we do next?"

"With one stop on the way, I think."

nine

ON A BRIGHT clear cold Tuesday morning, I climbed the back slope of the ridge. Surf tumbled in, making a continuous roar against the rock. I reached and grasped the small trunk of a wind-dwarfed tree and pulled myself up to where I could look over the top. In my surprise I nearly ducked back out of sight. I had not expected the Chipmann sun deck to be so close. I looked down into it at about a thirty-degree angle. Perhaps that made it seem closer. But it was, I judged, three hundred feet away. It was a special irony that there should be a nude woman on the sun terrace. She was prone on a faded blue sun pad. The wall shielded her from some of the west wind, and she had set up an additional wind screen, one of those made of a shining metal to intensify the heat of the sun. She was of heroic dimension, a redoubtable female, body brown as coffee beans, hair bleached to hemp, thighs like beer kegs, shoulders like Sonny Liston. I assumed she had to be Mrs. Chipmann, the dear friend who loaned Carl their house for celebrity assignation. It seemed odd to see the sun terrace in such vivid colors after seeing it so many times in black and white. Her face was turned toward me. She wore sunglasses. There was a half glass of tomato juice on the cement next to the sun pad.

There was absolutely no other place from which the terrace could be watched. She had every reason to think herself unobserved. I eased back, out of sight and turned and looked down. I could see part of the rear end of our pale gray Avis car parked in the cut where I had left it. I looked around at the immediate area. It was nonsensical to expect to find anything, after a year and a half. But find something I did. It was tucked down into a cleft of stone as if someone had wadded it and wedged it there, a small crumpled cardboard container, once yellow, now bleached pulpy white by sun and rain and weather. I could make out ghost writing on it, white on white. Kodak—Plus-X Pan.

I took it down with me and handed it to Dana as I got behind the wheel. She frowned at it, then saw what it was. She looked at me with a strange expression. "Why should this make it more real? God, could anything be more real than those pictures? But this is . . . like archeology, sort of. It's more . . . first hand."

"Don't get hooked on the feeling, Dana. Investigation can be a disease."

"It's a spooky feeling. I don't think I like it. It's unfair in a way, Travis. People get so exposed. It dwarfs people, doesn't it? By dwarfing them, it makes you feel bigger. Is that the fascination?"

"I don't know."

"But it *does* fulfill you in some way, doesn't it?"

"Let's drop it, shall we?"

"I'm sorry. I didn't realize it was a sore . . ."

"Shall we?"

"Alright!"

I drove swiftly southward with the sulks and with a silent woman. Ever since the popularization of the Freud Fraud, we are all addicted to fingering ourselves to see where it hurts, Mommy. With no one to kiss and make well.

So what if I am hooked on the hunt? All it does is make an orderly life untenable. You trade the kiddies and fireside and regular promotions and appointment to the house committee or the greens committee for a few, a very few, clear clean moments of a savage satisfaction akin to joy. And maybe in the process you keep a little essential privacy. Our dear Uncle owns over 23,000 polygraphs. Lie detectors. God alone knows how many industry owns. Not satisfied anymore with giving you the whole series of Multiphasic Personality Inventory tests, they want to make damn well certain you are not merely giving them the answers you think they want. They want to nail you into your permanent box right now, brother. Get in and lie still, and forty years from now we'll bury you.

I get this crazy feeling. Every once in a while I get it. I get the feeling that this is the last time in history when the offbeats like me will have a chance to live free in the nooks and crannies of the huge and rigid structure of an increasingly codified society. Fifty years from now I would be hunted down in the street. They would drill little holes in my skull and make me sensible and reliable and adjusted.

I am, to put it as bitterly as possible, a romantic. I know a windmill when I see one, by God, and I sneer at my white horse. It was appropriate that Lysa Dean should be the damsel in distress. She is such a sweet kid.

"Anyway," I said aloud, "she projects the image of a sweet kid."

Dana was inert for about two seconds, nodding her head, and then she gave a little jump and stared at me. "Don't *do* that!"

"Do what?"

"Get inside my head like that! How did you know what I was thinking?"

"I didn't."

She looked dubious. I glanced at her a few times when I could take my eyes off that languorous and lethargic California traffic. And somehow all of a sudden we were closer. Maybe it is like the learning curve, shaped like a profile of a stairway. We both knew something had happened and didn't know what it was. Her face colored and she turned away. I couldn't really *see* her any more. That was another clue. I could remember meeting a darkhaired strong-featured composed woman. A stranger. This was not she. This was Dana. Somebody else. Dana's eyes, Dana's mouth, Dana's hair and ears and body. Individual and unique and not related in any way to anyone previously known. Dana of the dear crooked tooth.

Santa Rosita was a stunted version of the Santa Barbara code of existence. Three industries, electronics, plastics and tourists, and squeeze the bejaysus out of all three. It was sharing the big boom-boom. The incomparably dull tract houses, glitteringly new, were marching out across the hills, cluttered with identical station wagons, identical children, identical barbecues, identical tastes in flowers and television. You see, Virginia, there really is a Santa Rosita, full of plastic people, in plastic houses, in areas noduled by the vast basketry of their shopping centers. But do not blame them for being so tiresome and so utterly satisfied with themselves. Because, you see, there is no one left to tell them what they are and what they really should be doing.

The dullest wire services the world has ever seen fill their little monopoly newspapers with self-congratulatory pap. Their radio is unspeakable. Their television is geared to a minimal approval by thirty million of them. And anything thirty million people like, aside from their more private functions, is bound to be bad. Their schools are group-adjustment centers, fashioned to shame the rebellious. Their churches are weekly votes of confidence in God. Their politicians are enormously likable, never saying a cross word. The goods they buy grow increasingly more shoddy each year, though brighter in color. For those who still read, they make do, for the most part, with the portentous gruntings of Uris, Wouk, Rand and others of that same witless ilk. Their magazine fare is fashioned by nervous committees.

You see, dear, there is no one left to ask them a single troublesome question. Such as: Where have you been and where are you going and is it worth it.

They are the Undisturbed. The Sleep-Lovers.

And they fill out an enormous number of forms every year, humbly and sincerely. Each one is given a number to use all his life.

Are they going to be awakened with a kiss? They feel vaguely uneasy about their young. My God, why can't these kids appreciate this best of all possible worlds? What's wrong with these restless punks? These . . . these goddam *drop-outs!*

Virginia, dear, through the strange alchemy of the gods, there are a disproportionate number of kids coming along these days with IQ's that are soaring toward a level too high to measure. These kids have very cold eyes. They are the ones who, one day, will stop playing with transistors, diodes and microcircuitry and look at Barrentown and start asking the rude questions. Or build a machine that will ask.

In the meanwhile, Virginia, Santa Rosita still exists, and it is as if some cynical genius had designed a huge complex penal colony in the sunshine, eliminating the need for guard towers and barbed wire by merely beaming a gigantic electronic message at the inmates, day and night, saying, You are in heaven! Be happy! If you can't be happy there, you

can't be happy anywhere! Vote! Consume! Donate! And
don't forget to use your number.

We drove in from the north at four in the afternoon of
that first Tuesday in March, and I checked us into two singles
in a chain motel—architecture: Lubratorium Moderne. She
wanted to call Miss Dean, and I wanted to try the number
for Mendez. After a small and cautious hesitation, I decided
not to put it through the motel switchboard. Caution can
be a way of life. Never leave anything which can be traced,
when you do have a choice.

A clear-voiced girl said, "Gallagher, Rosen and Mendez.
Good afternoon."

"Uh . . . may I speak with Mr. Mendez, please."

"One moment, sir."

"Good afternoon. This is Mr. Mendez' secretary. May I
help you?"

"I would like to speak with Mr. Mendez, please."

"He's on another line. May I call you back, or would you
like to hold?"

I held. I riffled the phone book with my free hand. They
were attorneys.

"Yes? Hello?" Mendez said in an impatient and harried
voice.

"Sorry to bother you. We need an address for the next of
kin for D. C. Ives."

"Who is we?"

"Keller Photo, sir. We had a lens for repair. It was under
the guarantee, but it took a long time. It had to go back to
the factory in Germany, no charge of course, and now
we . . ."

"Miss Trotter? Give this fellow Jocelyn Ives' address."

I heard him hang up. "Hello?" Miss Trotter said. "Just a
moment, please." She was back on the line quickly. "Have
you a pencil? Miss Jocelyn Ives, 2829 Appleton Way. Phone
765-3192. Have you got that?"

"Thanks. When did Ives die anyway?"

"Oh, just a few days before Christmas. He held on longer
than they thought he could, you know. Days and days, with
all that terrible brain damage. It's such a shame. He was *so*
talented."

"Well, that's the way it goes."

"I hope they find them some day."

"Don't we all. Thanks, Miss Trotter."

I started out of the phone booth, and then went back in and tried the number she gave me. It rang three times. A woman answered. "Is Georgie around?" I asked.

"You've the wrong number, I expect," she said. I thanked her and hung up. I walked thoughtfully back to the room. I knew that accent. It sounds cockney but isn't. It is Australian.

Dana had just finished talking to Lysa Dean. Miss Dean reported success with the promotion and a good audience response to *Winds of Chance* on premiere night. She was off soon, with group, to New York for additional promo work, panel shows and so on, four days there and then to Chicago.

I reported what I had learned, and added what I could guess. Dana looked more intrigued than shocked. "Killed, eh?"

"So it would seem."

"He was in a dangerous line of work."

"The quickest way is to give that sister a try."

"Can I come with you?"

"I might strike out. I'll try it alone. Then you can try from another angle."

Appleton Way was dead end. Truck terminals were edging closer to it. Nearby blocks were being leveled for some unimaginable improvement. But the street still had an illusion of peace. It contained multiple housing, old garden courts of pseudo-Moorish styling, faded citrus-tone paint on old stucco. 2829 was one of the larger complexes, and her door was off an arched open corridor along the side. A dark door opening into the gloom of a small apartment with too few windows. She looked at me through the six-inch gap the safety chain allowed, and I saw that she was perhaps daughter rather than sister.

"What do you want?"

You have to have a flair for it, an immediate and unthinking appraisal of the vulnerabilities. This one was wary and haughty. I could see that she was a big pale girl, Alice through a strange looking-glass. A twenty-year-old spinster. There are such. A big awkward fatty body in an unlovely jumper. A child face. Reddened nostrils. Pale heavy lips.

"I want to be sure you are Jocelyn Ives. Is there anything you could show me to prove it?" I kept my voice confidential.

"Why should I bother?"

"You do have the same accent."

"Who are you? What do you want?"

"I was associated with him in a certain venture quite a long time ago. I came here to make contact, and I just found out he's dead."

She gnawed her lip and then, to my utter astonishment, gave me a huge conspiratorial wink. She closed the door, unlatched the chain and opened it wide. "Please come in," she said heartily. When she had closed the door behind us, she said, "I do understand why you can't give me your name."

"Uh ... that's good."

"Back through here. The place is a mess. I'm off work today." I followed her along the murky hallway into a small living room. It was crowded with furniture too large and too expensive for the small apartment. Every surface was covered with large photographic prints, and scores of them were on the floor and leaning against the furniture and the walls. Many of them were matted. With clumsy awkward haste she cleared two chairs. "Do sit down. I've been sorting out. Lens Lab . . . that's a local hobby group . . . they want to put on a show of his best work. At the library. There are so *many*. I get quite confused."

"I can see how you would. It looks like fine work."

"Oh yes! That's my responsibility now, to see that everyone learns how good Father was. I am going to set up a traveling show also. And there is some interest in Rochester, of course."

"Of course."

She sat facing me and knotted her hands together and said, "I have been so hoping that *somebody* would show up. It's been so terribly difficult for me."

"I suppose it has."

"Poor Mr. Mendez has been doing his best to get everything straightened out for tax purposes. But having quite a large amount of cash turn up has sort of complicated things. And, of course, I couldn't explain the cash. Not to him. If it was supposed to be for necessary expenses, I'm sorry. It's all tied up now with courts and tax people and things. I will get it eventually, I imagine, or whatever part of it they don't take. At least the house can be sold. You know, I have been hoping someone would show up. And you look almost exactly like the kind of man I pictured."

"What can I do for you?"

"I kept my mouth shut, as Father would have wished. And I guess I do not really have to have any posthumous glory for him. He said that was the thing none of you could ever expect. He taught me to be very careful and discreet about . . . the contacts, and not to ask him questions. I have been wondering if you could go to Mr. Mendez and explain to him the sort of work Father was doing for you. I think it might make the estate work easier."

"I'm sorry. I have no authority to do that."

"I was afraid so," she said. "Oh dear. And the ridiculous police will have to go right on thinking it was just someone after his pocket money?"

"I'm afraid so."

She studied me. "Really, how do I know you are what I think you are?"

"We don't carry that sort of identification."

"I suppose not. It wouldn't be very safe, I expect." She looked uneasy. "But why wouldn't you have known he was dead?"

"I've been out of touch."

I now had the shape of it all. There was something unwholesome about her, a greasy sheen to her flesh, a soiled smell in the dark little apartment. But she was his loved daughter. Blackmail needed a cover story. Perhaps it had been her guess at first, that Father was in some sort of patriotic undercover work, and when she faced him with it, it was easiest to go along. And, of course, the Enemy had slain him.

I had to find the right way to open her up. I leaned toward her and said, "Jocelyn, I think I can promise you that some day it can all be told."

Tear tracks like the sidewalk marks of snails gleamed on the round pale cheeks, and she made a froggy sobbing sound. . . .

ten

I LIKED THE way Dana listened. She felt no compulsion to fill a silence with questions. She knew there was more to come. I could not see her distinctly. She sat over by the motel windows in darkness. The light was at my elbow, gleaming on the silver cup.

"Ives liked to live well," I said. "He did free-lance photography in Melbourne. Fashion, news breaks, everything. A Hollywood outfit made a movie over there. He got permission to work on the set. His stills were apparently damned good. The stars liked them. The studio brought him over. That was eight years ago. She was twelve. He had about four years of it, and did pretty well. And lived well. Then something went wrong. I guess he got himself on that little blacklist they have. I don't imagine it is important to know what cooked him. The girl says it was jealousy. His work was too good. He moved up here to Santa Rosita. His studio was in his home. Weddings, parties, awards, portraits. A nice cover story. She thinks he had some other base in the city. She's so proud of him. Proud of that cynical son of a bitch with his sports cars and fine house and housekeeper."

I got up and collected both silver cups and fixed us another.

"She showed me the clippings. He went on a trip. She doesn't know where. He was gone two days. He came back to the house. He went out again and said he would be back within the hour. That was ten in the evening last December tenth. They found his car, locked, on Verano Street. He was found about a hundred feet away, dragged behind a

102

warehouse, with the top of his skull smashed in, pockets empty, watch gone. They thought he would be dead on arrival, but the heart kept beating for five days. As far as the girl knows, they haven't a clue. Nobody knows what he was doing in that neighborhood. It's mostly industrial small time, empty at night.

After a long silence she said, "Did he leave her anything?"

"Small insurance. The equity in the house. About thirty-eight thousand in cash, already impounded while they check his tax returns. Then a lot of cameras, studio equipment, dark room equipment, huge stacks of arty photographs."

She asked me if I was certain about Ives. I'd been saving it for her. I told her how I'd wormed it out of the girl. "So his loving daughter was the one who helped him operate that drop and flashed the green light at you to toss the money out."

Dana shook her head slowly. "And I imagined horrible hoodlums out there . . . and it was that poor simple girl helping Daddy in his spy business. What a total bastard he must have been, to endanger her so!"

And I thought wistfully how easy it would have been for Lysa Dean to have busted it up in the beginning, before it got off the ground. "Ives could trust his daughter," I explained. "And he didn't have to split with her, and she didn't even know what was in the packages. He used her the same way, with variations, on other projects."

"Loyal little helper," Dana said. "Just like me."

"Let's go eat."

She put her sweater on. At the door she stopped me and said, "Trav, you didn't give her any little suspicion that . . . all was not what it seemed?"

"When I left, I told her she could be proud of Daddy. She stood tall and the tears dripped off her fat chin."

She squeezed my arm. In the outside lights, her dark eyes were shiny. "Soft as butter," she said.

"The arm?"

"Idiot, your darn arm is like a slab of redwood. I just meant I'm glad you left her that much."

"I wonder how long she'll keep it."

"What do you mean?"

"Somebody killed him. If they find him, he might have all the right reasons. I think I might talk to a cop."

"Why, dear?" she asked earnestly.

"Dear?"

"Oh, shut up! It was just a . . . reflex."

"You've done it twice today."

"Why will you talk to a cop?"

"Because they very probably know a little more than Miss Ives thinks they know. And we're close to the heart of it now, Dana. Where did D.C. Ives' file copies go?"

My man was Sergeant Starr. Bill Starr. He was a little fellow about forty, very jaunty and bouncy. He was twenty percent nose, and it looked as if that nose had been hit at least once from every possible direction. Under the nose was the abrupt curve of an amiable little smile. He was a clowner, a most happy fellow. He seemed to want you to like him. There was so much nose, there was a danger of misreading the eyes. They were small, cat yellow, and about as soft and mild as cross sections of brass rod.

His tidy little gray office had a rack for cups won in various skills. Several of them were for pistol. He bounced up and perched on the corner of his desk and beamed at me and said, "Why should I play games with anybody, pal? Am I in a buyer's market? Maybe, for residents. If I want to keep a source going. Sure. But I can park your gray tired ass in the tank and keep you there until you get eager to please."

I chuckled as merrily as he and said, "This friend I'm doing the favor for would be terribly upset. No influence here at all, of course. Except the kind of lawyers money will buy. Platoons of them, if need be. I have no record, Sergeant. But careless people have put me in from time to time, here and there. And I have been hit on the head by old-fashioned ones. So it would be an inconvenience for both of us. I'm eager to please right now. And eager to have you please me."

He picked the assorted cards and licenses off his desk and handed them to me. "McGee, there is every identification here except the right one."

"Cards are needed to do a favor for a friend?"

"I'll tell you again. If you have official status then *maybe* you can protect your client. But you have nothing. You *have* to tell me who hired you!"

"But I told you, Sergeant, that we might get around to that, if things go well. Besides, I'm not hired. It's just . . ."

"Oh God yes. A favor for a friend." He reached for his hat. "Let's try some coffee."

He drew a car from the pool and we went ten blocks to a drive-in. The pretty waitress knew him by name, and brought us coffee and raised doughnuts.

"I'll start," I said. "D.C. Ives. Sometimes a man has to be killed before people get the idea of some kind of hanky-panky."

"Hanky-panky. Now isn't that sweet! Put it this way. It isn't a legal requirement a man should have a checking account, but nearly everybody with forty-thousand-dollar homes does. An estimate of his take on a legit basis would be fifty or sixty a week. Living expenses better than a thousand a month. So he could be living off a big score from way back, or making little scores as he goes along."

"He was making it as he went along."

"Thanks a lot. I already figured that."

"Did you figure how?"

"It's your turn again, McGee."

"He had a studio and darkroom in his house, and he also had another setup. I'd guess somewhere near Verano Street. A limited setup. A quality enlarger for 35mm, a setup for making and drying eight by ten prints, no automation for quantity production—almost what you'd expect of an advanced amateur, a one-man operation."

"To do what?"

"Isn't it your turn, Sergeant?"

"Okay. He would do there something he wouldn't want to do home on account of his daughter. When she wasn't in school, she helped him with the home setup. He did a lot of traveling. Short trips. Assignments, he called them. I say it wasn't just a standard smut shop. The requirements in that field are too low. And the pay is low. What do you say it was, McGee?"

"Discreet, careful, expert blackmail. Plus maybe some industrial espionage. And maybe just the long shots of people with the wrong people—the executive talking to the competition, the banker with the tout. Long lens stuff, up and down this coast. How would he get the work? Some from legitimate agencies, maybe. Some from the great unwashed. With really juicy negatives, he could wring a lot of money out, if the people were important."

"And eventually make a slip and get his head smashed in."

"Probably."

"McGee, if you are trying to do a favor for a friend by getting hold of prints or negatives, forget it."

"They're gone?"

"If he'd been killed immediately, maybe we'd have moved a little faster. We found his hidey-hole. A warehouse corner with its own entrance. It was an area check that turned it up. His prints were on everything. Not much file space for prints, but it was stone empty. No negatives. The file had been locked, and it was pried open. The door had been unlocked and relocked with a key. A good lock. There was a tin money box in the back of the file. It was busted open too."

"What are you holding back, Starr?"

"Me? Me!"

"So all right. My friend is a sick sad girl. She's at Hope Island on Bastion Key in Florida. Her name is Nancy Abbott. She's a drunk. She's been at that retreat for months. Her rich architect daddy is dying, or dead by now, in San Francisco. Ives sneaked some nasty pictures of her a year and a half ago. Now give me the rest."

"I can check that out. The rest? Okay, I found out beyond any doubt that the break-in wasn't accomplished until the day *after* Ives was clobbered. And in Ives' pocket was a key to his little lab. Ives had an employee. Semi-retarded. Samuel Bogen, age 46. On and off welfare for years. Trouble twenty years ago. Peeping Tom and indecent exposure, and about four ninety-day falls for that. From what I can find out, Ives used him for scut work, paying him a dollar an hour for washing trays, drying prints, that sort of thing. By the time we got a line on him, Bogen had dropped off the face of the earth. He could be just a harmless spook. Or he could have flipped and bashed his boss. We think we traced him onto a Los Angeles bus. We've had an alert out on him ever since. Medium height, medium weight, glasses, bad teeth, hair brown turning gray, no special identifying marks or characteristics. No family. Left no lead behind in his furnished room three blocks off Verano Street. There is another thing too that makes me less interested in him. At about the right time, a car left the area at high speed. Bogen apparently never owned a car and doesn't drive."

I couldn't risk pursuing the Bogen matter further. I was afraid the little tiger would check it back and come up with Lysa Dean's name.

"So who was involved in the Abbott girl's pictures?" he demanded.

I was ready for that one. "A stock car driver named Sonny Catton. He was killed last year when he hit a wall."

"Where were the pictures taken?"

"Up around Point Sur someplace, at a private home I think."

"A year and a half ago, you said? So why the heat to get them back now?"

"She was worried about whether he was using them to blackmail her dying father."

"How did you track it back to this Ives?"

"Sergeant, that's a long long story. Let me ask you one. Suppose somebody had some work for Ives. They couldn't get him. So they called Mendez, of Gallagher, Rosen and Mendez, and found out from Mendez he was dead. Does that mean anything?"

"I wondered about that too. Charlie Mendez is clean. Small services for small fees. Like having mail come there."

"Summation, Sergeant?"

"Who, me? Okay, D.C. Ives was very shifty and clever and careful. But one night he forgot to be careful and one of his pigeons got to him. When Bogen heard his boss was dying, he used his own key to get in. He took the dirty pictures and the money and ran."

"So that makes it a dead end for me, Sergeant."

"Are you sure?"

"It was just a favor for a friend."

eleven

WE LEFT EARLY Thursday morning and drove down to the city, to Lysa Dean's canyon home, secluded behind an impressive pink wall. The staff was cut down to one Korean couple, maid and gardener. When he recognized Dana, he smiled broadly and unlocked the big metal gates for us. It was a hot day. The wall enclosed about one acre. A Mexican architect had done the house for her and the third husband. I guess you could call it Cuernavaca Aztec.

Dana showed me around. The plantings were splendid. The pool was drained. The dogs had been boarded. Walking through the silence of terrazzo, puffy white rugs, dark paneling removed from ancient churches, I counted five full-length oil portraits of the owner. And not one of an ex-husband.

Dana wanted to get different clothes. She showed me how she was set up. A small functional suite opposite the service area, with a rather stark bedroom, a large and luxurious bath, a small tidy office with a row of large gray filing cabinets, a battleship desk. There was a picture in the bedroom, Dana, younger, glowing, intense—holding the new baby in her arms. A young man with a homely, crooked, likable face was staring down at the child too, his arm around his wife.

She saw me glance at it and said, too imperatively, "Please wait for me out there in the office. This won't take a minute."

On an office shelf I saw bound, gold-lettered scripts for the Lysa Dean movies. *Winds of Chance* was among them. I took it down and opened it at random. It seemed highly improbable to me that anyone, living or dead, had ever said lines like that.

I put the script back on the shelf and paced restlessly. There were loose ends. A lot of them. But I could not see how they were pertinent to what I'd been asked to do. I couldn't recover any of the money Lysa Dean had paid Ives.

It seemed reasonably evident that Bogen had gone into business for himself. His note to Lysa sounded as Starr had described him. He would have picked up a few crude lab techniques from Ives. If the police had been looking for him for three months without success, I didn't have much chance of reaching out and picking him up.

We could fly east and catch Lysa in New York. Make a report. Working a complaint through normal police channels, we could get all there was in the files on Bogen. The people responsible for protecting the star could be alerted to watch for anybody who might be Bogen. If she insisted, maybe we could work out a way to trap him, using her as bait. With a little bit of judgment and a lot of luck, I had pushed it about as far as I could.

I could make a few guesses. Bogen had fled with a good piece of money and a whole stack of unpleasant pictures, and holed up, perhaps in Los Angeles. He'd fled on December 6th. Those pictures could seriously upset an already disturbed mind. It was highly unlikely that he could have lifted any neat little list of names and addresses. Maybe the pictures covered quite a few of Ives' quiet ventures. If Bogen wanted to get cute with anyone, he would be restricted to those faces he could recognize. Maybe there were a few more celebrity faces in the stack. What was the time sequence? In early January, a month after he fled Santa Rosita, he was out in Las Vegas leaving off the package for Lysa Dean at the desk at The Sands. The columns would have located her for him. No further contact in two months. Was he busy bugging some other famous people who had been captured by Ives' sneaky lens? Was he waiting for Lysa Dean to come back to the Los Angeles area?

At any rate, it would be a comfort to her to know the kind of nut who was running around with pictures that could ruin her, to know his name and his appearance. She would have to decide what that much was worth. I'd dug a pretty good hole in the expense money.

Ives' murderer was none of my business. The list of possibilities would have to be as long as my arm.

But I didn't like the way this one was ending. And I couldn't see Lysa Dean being ecstatic about it either.

Dana came out of her bedroom. She wore a pretty green outfit, and carried her repacked suitcase. She said, too cheerfully, "Are we ready?"

She seemed very tense. I went and took the suitcase from her. With a quaver in her cheerful voice, she said, "This place gets on my nerves. It never did before. I don't know why. I feel as if I hardly know the Dana Holtzer who lives here. I expect her to come in and ask me who the hell I am."

"Watch out for her. A very icy broad."

She paused in the doorway to look at me, her expression at once vulnerable and wary. "Travis?"

"Yes, honey."

"I can't take too much change. So please don't. Things that get brittle . . . they break, you know."

"I like you. That's all it is."

She nodded. "But we have laughed too much. Do you understand that?"

"I understand that. And you'll be back in harness tonight."

"That picture you saw in there. Did it explain anything?"

"I could have drawn it from memory before I even saw it. You don't have to be explained to me. I don't have to make adjustments with you and to you. Hell with it. Let's go get on our airplane." I tilted her chin up, kissed the corner of her mouth closest to the crooked tooth. A little peck, like cousins. So she smiled, and one tear spilled, and I followed her in flight, clackety-whack across terrazzo, green skirt whipping, powerful calves clenching, back very straight and head held high.

We had twenty minutes before they called the flight. Our gear was checked aboard. Early afternoon. I bought a paper. I was scanning it. The name jumped out at me from a small item on page one of the second section. Casino employee slain in Las Vegas. Patricia Davies bludgeoned at doorstep of trailer last night. Once married to sportsman Vance M'Gruder.

Without a word I pointed it out and handed it to Dana. She looked at me, her eyes wide.

"I can't pass that up," I said. "It could be Sammy."

"But . . . our luggage is . . ."

"Dana, you go on to New York. Take care of my stuff at the other end. I'll check this out and be along."

"But I'm supposed to stay with you."

I took hold of her wrists and gave her a little shake. "You have to go to New York. You're a big girl. I don't have to draw diagrams for you. You and I have . . . run out of time."

She held my gaze and her mouth made the shape of that word. Time. Without making a sound. The strength in her face was softened. And younger. "Thank you," she said solemnly. "Thank you, Travis, for knowing when the time ran out."

I released her, turning away, saying, "Your boss expects you. So go ahead." She murmured something about arranging my ticket, and went off into the throng. I watched her go, and for an instant had in my mind the grotesque and unworthy image of the time when you feel the tarpon pick up speed for that last, great, heart-busting leap, and see him go high and see him, right at the peak of it, give that final snap of his head that throws your lure back into your lap. The image wasn't even accurate. I'd turned conservationist. I'd let the line go slack and said goodby.

I waited. And waited. Her flight was called. I went to the gate. I did not see her. I went to the airline desk. They checked the manifest for me. Slowly. Sir, the passenger canceled before flight time. I felt fear, worry, irritation. I had played the whole game too loosely, too confidently, and maybe somebody very fast and bright had moved out of the shadows.

I prowled the martian reaches of the terminal, searching for my girl in green. And found her, saw her through the glass front of a men's shop. I went striding in. A clerk was helping her. She gave me a startled and guilty look, then swung all that vivid force of personality upon me, saying, "Darling, I told you I'd forget the shirt sizes. It's *such* a damn nuisance losing luggage. Are these all right? Wash-and-wear, so we could make do with two, don't you think? But what size, dear?"

"Seventeen and a half, thirty-six," I said humbly.

"Two of these in that size, please. And you don't really mind stretch socks too much, do you? Size thirty-three shorts, mmm? No, don't wrap them. I can pop them right in here." She lifted the small suitcase up onto the counter, a cheap one of pale blue anodized aluminum. As she put the articles in, I got a glimpse of some feminine things, and some drug store parcels. She latched it and waited for her change.

"We've got a flight in about twenty-five minutes," she said.

I carried the case out of the store into the waiting room area. I carried it to a quiet space and put it down and turned to her and said, "Have you lost your fool mind?"

She locked strong icy fingers onto my wrist and looked up at me and said, "It's all right. Really. It's all right."

"But . . ."

"I couldn't get the luggage back. It was stowed aboard. It'll be taken care of in New York. Look. I've been a grownup for a long time."

"It's just that . . ."

"Shut up, darling. Shut up, shut up, shut up. Do you want me to draw pictures for you? Stop looking like a spavined moose. Say you're glad. Say something."

I put fingertips on her cheek, ran my thumb along the black gloss of her eyebrow. "Okay. Something."

She closed her eyes and shivered. "Oh God. No claims, Trav. Nothing like that. Either way."

"Either way."

"Just don't laugh."

"You know better than that."

I read consternation in her expression. "Maybe I'm just not what you . . . Maybe you never really . . . You could have been just being polite and now . . ."

"You know better than that too. Shut up, dear."

"I wired New York."

"Kindly excuse delay."

"Dammit, we've never even really kissed. My knees are all wobbly and strange. Please lead me to a drink, darling."

During the flight, in spite of all the persuasive immediate magic of Girl, in spite of scent, closeness, dark eyes to drown in, and the shallow-breathed feeling of expectancy, the workman part of my mind kept moving in old and seamy patterns. We'd made a big swing, and, one by one, we'd been dropping them out of the final count. Carl Abelle, terror of the ski lifts, dangerous as a prat fall on a bunny slope. Sonny Catton, cooked meat in a pretty whoosh and bloom of high octane. Nancy Abbott, cooked just as thoroughly but over a lower flame. No point in checking Harvey and Richie, the Cornell kids. Their biggest problem was to find someone, anyone, who would ever believe their story. Caswell Edgars was out of it. And out of just about everything else in the world too. Ives was gone, and violently. So was Patty M'Gruder. If old Abbott, Nancy's father, had any luck left, he was dead by now too. Less violently but less pleasantly. It was narrowing down. To a yacht bum named Vance M'Gruder, to a waitress named Whippy, to a retarded little man named Bogen. It was like going through an empty house, checking the closets. Either it was more complex than I could comprehend, or so it made even less sense. But there was a nastiness somewhere in it that was out of control. I sensed that, and sensed it was aimed at Lysa Dean, and maybe at me, and I couldn't imagine who or how. I knew only two things. I was running out of closets. And I was glad I hadn't been at that house party. So I held the hand of the girl, and told myself it was a fine world, and filed away my doom-thoughts.

A bored kid built a shiny little model city with his new kit and when it was finished he gave it one hell of a kick and spewed bit hunks of it out across the desert floor. We tilted down across the afternoon, seeing an unreality of blue pools and green fairways against that old lizard-skin brown of the everlasting desert. We came in with a batch of pilgrims —the brand-new ones trying to be cool about their interest in the air terminal slots, about all the hawking and proclaiming and loud instant promotions. All the old pilgrims wore the memory of pain, and were impatient to get to that certain table at that certain place, in time for crucifixion. I noticed a pair of appraisers as our group came through the gate, backs against the wall, staring left and right, somnolently vigilant, bouncing the little black glances off the pilgrims like aimed bb shot. They have the index memories of the ten thousand faces in disrepute in Slotsville, plus a feel for new trouble on the way—the ones who have come to get it any way they can, including using a gun on the winners. My lady performed no transit services this time. It was a fine and pleasant distinction related to the absolute silence of the airplane ride, the hand tightly held, the dark eyes hooded. She stood four square, still and humble, patient and sensuous, while I, with no bag to retrieve, went off to dicker a vehicle and, with ironic impulse, took that most typical of game-town cars, a big airconditioned convertible, this one in metallic blue-green, white leather, ominously silent as Forest Lawn.

There had been a place I liked, way out on the Strip, an utterly gameless and consequently expensive motor house called the Apache, and I knew it would be meaningless and would astonish her should I consult her. At the desk I said I had been there before, knew I wanted a double cabana at the pool, gave the porter a dollar to let me have the key and find my own way.

It was a great long room in gold and green, with two huge beds, all of it too bright in the dazzle of poolside sun. I pulled the cords that creaked the heavy yellow draperies across the acre of window wall, turning the room into a shadowy gloom of gold. The whisper of the hushed cooled air made it an oasis, a thousand years from yesterday, and ten thousand years from tomorrow. Every fifth breath she took was very deep, with a little catch, like a hiccup at the high end. I put my hands upon her, at waist and nape of neck, stopping her sleepy sway. The man who sits in the steel office and throws the switches and pushes the buttons can rest his hand on his desk and feel, more like a low-cycle sound than any measurable vibration, the power that thrums in the bowels of the light plant. She felt unyielding and I could not guess how it would be for us. Then she gave a little crooked sigh, turned her mouth upward to me, leaned with heat and softness and purpose.

There is one kind of rightness that is an almost-rightness, because it is merciless and total and ends in a deathlike lethargy.

Then there is another kind of almost-rightness that can never be finished.

Both of these make you strangers to each other. Both of these things make you untidily anxious to give and receive reassurances.

But with Dana it was that rare and selfless rightness which moves with but the gentlest hiatus from one completion to the next, each a growth in knowing and closeness while, unheeded, the deep sweet hours go by. After all the fierceness is gone, it then astonishes by returning in that last time which ends it without question for now, and she is spent and dies there, slumbrous and fond.

I fought sleep. I made myself get up. I covered her over and went and showered and dressed. I turned on a meager light in the room and sat on the bed, pushed black curls aside, kissed the sweet nape of a musky neck. She turned to peer up at me, her face soft and emptied and young. "Yuhraw dress!" she mumbled in accusation.

"I'm going out for a little while. You sleep, honey."

She tried to frown. "Y'be careful, d'ling."

"Love you," I said. It doesn't cost a thing. Not when you do. I kissed a soft and smiling mouth, and I think she was asleep before I stood up. I left the low light on and let myself out.

I walked toward the main buildings feeling all that strange ambivalence of the conquering male. Goaty self-esteem, slight melancholy, a mildly pleasant and unfocused guilt, a tin-soldier strut.

But something more than that with her. A feeling of achieving and establishing identities, hers and mine.

There had been no dishonesties. And so, in all that total giving and taking, I had been aware of her as Dana, so vital and so enduring. The slight physical strangeness of the very beginning of it had lasted but a very short time. Then she was all known and dear. As if we had been apart for a very long time and found each other again, quickly getting over the awkwardness of separation.

After that it was a knowing and re-knowing in a profound way which has no words. It became a symbolic dialogue. I give thee. I take thee. I prize thee.

And there was also the fatuous feeling of enormous luck. It is such a damned blind chance after all.

I worked my way through two bemused gin and bitters while they seared my steak. Over coffee I stopped marveling at myself and got a local paper and read the more detailed account of the murder of Patty M'Gruder.

Then I drove downtown and parked and wandered through that strange area of cut-rate stores, pastel marriage chapels, open-sided casinos bathed in a garish fluorescence. Spooks trudged amid the tourists, and the cops kept a close sharp watch. Old ladies yanked at the handles, playing their dimes out of paper cups. Music bashed across the dry night air, in conflict with itself, and in the noisier alcoves one could buy anything from a dream book to a plastic bird turd.

The Four Treys was a long bright narrow jungle of machinery. What happened to the old-fashioned slot machine? Now you can pull two handles, hit three space ships and an astronaut and get a moon-pot, which is one and a half jack pots. The change girls sat behind wire, popping open the paper cylinders of silver, dumping it into paper cups for the people. At regular intervals came the clash of money into the scoop, and a shrillness of joy.

I had just wanted a look. I needed no directions. Presently I got back behind the wheel of the luxury device afforded me by a famous movie star and drove off again through the neoned night.

twelve

THE TRAILER PARK was called Desert Gate. I had to go down through town and out the far side to get to it. It was a little after ten o'clock when I got there. Some orderly soul had set it up with the requirement that all trailers be parked in herringbone array on either side of a broad strip of asphalt going nowhere. The entrance was an aluminum arch, tall and skinny, with a pink floodlight on it.

The trailers were large, all snugged down off their wheels, with little patios and screened porches added. About half of them were dark. Patricia had lived—and died in front of—the sixth one on the left. It was lighted. I parked and went to the porch door. As I raised a hand to bang on the aluminum frame, a big woman appeared, silhouetted in the inner doorway.

"Whatya want?"

"I want to talk to Martha Whippler."

"Who are you?"

"The name is McGee. I was a friend of Patty's."

"Look, why don't you go away? The kid has had a hard day. She's pooped. Okay?"

"It's all right, Bobby," a frail voice said. "Let him in."

As I went in, the big woman stood back out of the way. When I saw her in the light I realized she was younger than I had thought. She wore jeans and a blue work shirt, sleeves rolled high over brown heavy forearms. Her hair was brown and cropped short and she wore no makeup. The interior was all pale plywood paneling, vinyl tile, glass curtains, plastic upholstery, stainless steel. A slight girl lay on a day

117

bed, propped up on pillows, long coppery hair tousled around her sad wan face. Her eyes were red. Her lipstick was smeared. She had a drink in her hand. She wore a very frilly nylon robe. Though she was a lot slimmer, I knew her at once.

"Whippy!" I said, and then felt like a damn fool for not having figured it out.

It startled her. She stared at me with disapproval. "I don't know you. I don't remember you from anyplace. People call me Martha now. Pat wouldn't let them call me by my old name." There was something quite solemn and childlike about her. And vulnerable.

"I'm sorry. I'll call you Martha."

"What's your name?"

"Travis McGee."

"I never heard Pat say your name."

"I didn't know her well, Martha. I know a few other people you might know. Vance. Cass. Carl. Nancy Abbott. Harvey. Richie. Sonny."

She sipped her drink, frowning at me over the rim of the glass. "Sonny is dead. I heard that. I heard that he burned up, and it didn't mean a thing to me."

"Nancy saw him burn."

She looked incredulous. "How could that happen?"

"She was traveling with him then."

She shook her head in slow wonder. "Her traveling with him. Oh boy. Who could imagine that. Me, sure. But her? Gee, it doesn't seem possible, believe you me."

"Martha, I want to talk to you alone."

"I bet you do," the big girl behind me said.

"Mr. McGee, this is my friend Bobby Blessing. Bobby, whyn't you go away a while, okay?"

Bobby studied me. It is the traditional look they reserve for the authentic male, a challenging contempt, a bully-boy antagonism. There seem to be more of them around these days. Or perhaps they are merely bolder. The word is butch. Having not the penis nor the beard, they damn well try to have everything else. One of the secondary sex character- istics they seem to be able to acquire is the ballsy manner, the taut-shouldered swagger, the roostery go-to-hell attitude. They have a menacing habit of running in packs lately. And the unwary chap who tries to make off with one of their brides can get himself a stomping that stevedores would admire. These are a sub-culture, long extant, but recently emerged from hiding. In their new boldness they do a frightening job of recruiting, having their major successes among the vulnerable platoons of those meek girls who, like Martha Whippler, are abused by men, by the Catton-kind of man, used, abused, sickened, shared, frightened and . . . at last, driven into the camp of the butch.

"I'll be where I can hear you call me," Bobby said without taking her stony stare from my face. She went out, rolling her shoulders, hitching at her jeans.

I moved closer to Martha, and sat in a skeletal plastic chair half facing her. She looked down into her half of a drink and said, "You named the people that were there that time."

"And left one out?"

"That movie actress," she whispered.

"Have you told people about her being there?"

"Oh, nothing like that ever happened to me before. I couldn't *tell* anybody about it. I mean I could talk to Pat about it sometimes. You know. I used to have nightmares. She took me back home with her from there. I knew . . I always knew she would rather it was Nancy."

She looked wistful. She had a cheap, empty, pretty little face, eyebrows plucked to fine lines, mouth made larger with lipstick.

"Did you ever get to see the pictures?" I asked her.

Even the most vapid ones have an urchin shrewdness about them, the wariness of the consistently defensive posture.

"What pictures?"

"The ones Vance had taken."

"For hours and hours today they kept asking me questions, questions. How do I know you just aren't another smart guy?"

"I can't prove I'm not." I hesitated. She was suggestible. I wanted the right approach, without fuss. Grief made an additional vulnerability. Kindly ol' McGee seemed the best bet. I shook my head sadly. "I'm just a fellow who thinks Patricia got a very bad deal from Vance M'Gruder, very bad indeed."

Tears welled. She snuffled into her fist. "Oh God. Oh God yes. That bastard. That total bastard!"

"Some of us have never understood why Pat didn't fight it a little harder."

"Gee, you don't know what she had stacked against her.

That rotten Vance had been planning it a long time. He got some kind of morality report on her from the London police from way before they were married, I guess to show that she knew she shouldn't get married. And then he had the tape recorder things of her and Nancy at their house, and her and me at their house, and the pictures he hired that man to get, following them around. It must have cost an awful lot, the whole thing, but as Pat said, it was a hell of a lot cheaper than California divorce. She couldn't get a lawyer to agree to fight it. I mean, after all, there wasn't any question about the way she was."

"Did you get to see those pictures, Martha?"

"Oh sure. The funny thing, they made it look like nobody else was around at all. I don't know how that man got those pictures so close, Pat with me and with Nancy and with Lysa Dean, just one with Lysa Dean, one where you couldn't tell it was Lysa Dean unless you knew."

"So by the time you saw those pictures, you and Pat were together?"

"Yes. The rotten thing he did, we went up to the city to see some friends of hers, and we came back to Carmel, he was gone and the locks were changed, and our personal stuff was piled in a carport, and there was a man there to keep anybody from breaking in or anything. The way it was, she was still trying to get over being in love with Nancy, and maybe she never did. I guess maybe she never did get over it. But I did try to make her happy, I really did."

"Why would somebody want to kill her, Martha?"

She sobbed again, and blew her nose. "I don't *know!* I just don't *know.* That's what they kept asking me. Gee, we lived real quiet here, over a year now, and for a long time we've been working the same shift at the Four Treys, me as a drink waitress and her on a change booth. Just a few friends. She hadn't got interested in any other girl or anything, and nobody was after me like that. There was just one thing."

"What do you mean?"

She frowned and shook her head. "I don't know. It started weeks ago. Before that, whenever she'd think of Vance she'd go into a terrible rage, and sometimes she'd cry. Weeks ago she got a letter from somebody. She didn't let me see it and I can't find it so I guess she destroyed it. She was kind of . . . far away for a few days after she got it and she wouldn't tell me anything. Then one day when I was out, she made long-distance phone calls. She really ran up a terrible bill. Forty dollars and something. And later she made a few more calls. Then she got very pleased about something. She'd be grinning and humming around and I'd ask her why she felt so good and she'd say never mind. Sometimes she would grab me and dance me around and she'd tell me everything was going to be just fine, and we were going to be rich. It didn't matter so much to me. I mean we were doing all right here. We didn't *have* to be rich. I don't know if it had anything to do with her being murdered last night."

"Where were you when it happened?"

"I *heard* it! My God, I was in bed half asleep. I was sort of worrying about her. I've got a virus and I was off work. She was supposed to be finished at eleven and home by quarter past, but it was a little after midnight when I heard the car motor. I could tell it was ours, it's such a noisy little car. I'd left one light on for her. I wondered what she'd bring me. She'd bring me a little present if I was sick. Some kind of joke sort of. The car stopped out there and I heard the car door, and then just outside that screen door, she yelled 'What are you . . . ' Just those words. There was a kind of a terrible crunching sound. And a falling sound. And steps running. I turned on the lights and put my robe on and ran out and she was just ouside the door on the ground, and her head . . ."

I waited several minutes while she slowly and painfully pulled herself back together.

"She was so alive," Martha moaned.

"But several weeks ago she stopped being mad at Vance?"

"Yes. But I don't know what it means."

"After she was locked out of the house, she did have a chance to talk to her husband?"

"Oh, several times. She begged and pleaded."

"But it didn't do any good."

"He wouldn't even let her have her car. He said she was lucky to keep the clothes she'd bought. Finally he gave her five hundred dollars so she could afford to go away. I had about seventy-five dollars. We came here on a bus and got jobs. He was nasty to her."

"Martha, does the name Ives mean anything to you? D.C. Ives?"

She looked blank. "No."

"Santa Rosita?"

She tilted her empty little head. "That's strange!"

"What do you mean?"

"Just a couple of days ago she was singing that old song. Santa Lucia. But she was saying Rosita instead of Lucia, and I said she had it wrong and she laughed and said she knew she did. Why did you ask about that? I don't understand."

"Maybe it doesn't mean anything."

"But if it has anything to do with who killed her . . ."

"Did she have any kind of appointment coming up?"

"Appointment? Oh, I'd forgotten. Just the other day she said she might have to take a little trip. Alone. Just for a day or two. It made me jealous. She teased me and let me get real jealous, and then she said it was a kind of a business trip, and she'd tell me all about it later."

"Where was she going to go?"

"Phoenix. Gee, we don't know a soul in Phoenix."

"How soon was she going?"

"I don't know. It sounded as if she meant real soon."

I couldn't shake loose anything else of interest. She was worn out. But she was still alert enough to ask again who I was and what I wanted. I had to answer a question with a question.

"What are you going to do now, Martha?"

"I haven't thought about it."

"It's your chance to get out of . . . this kind of situation."

Her little mouth firmed up. "I don't know what you think you mean by that. Listen, Pat got me out of a lousy situation. I don't want anything like that again ever. What do you know about anything?"

"Don't get sore."

"Why shouldn't I? Jesus Christ! Anything you people don't understand, it has to be lousy. Pat always said that. The world doesn't have to be your way. We never asked anybody to approve or disapprove. It's our own business. Who did we hurt?"

"You?"

"Me! That's some joke. That really is. Honest to God, when I remember the way it used to have to be, when I thought that was the only thing there was, boy, it makes my stomach turn right over. I've got friends who want to take care of me."

"I bet you have."

She stared at me, narrowed her eyes, threw her head back and yelled, "Bobby! Bobby!"

I left without any particular haste, but without delay either. Even so, they were between me and my car. Bobby had a friend, equally sizable. In the angle of the light the friend looked like the young Joe DiMaggio, but with a black dutch bob, and wearing desert rat khakis. Joe carried a putter. The gold head and chrome shaft glittered.

They separated and moved in from either side.

"Don't make any stupid mistakes," I said, coming to a halt.

Joe had managed to train herself down to a good imitation of a baritone. "You bassars got to get a lesson not to come around here bothering the brides."

"What have you got here?" I asked. "A colony?"

"Smart ass," Bobby said as they moved in.

They generally do very well against the undoctrinated male. There is a chivalrous reluctance to hit a woman. Martha had come to the trailer doorway to watch the sport. I had learned a painful lesson long ago when reluctance had slowed reaction time, and I had spent the next several days walking around like an eighty-eight-year-old man. It is the type of mistake you are not likely to make twice in one lifetime. And these two were more dangerous than male thugs because their abberrations fired their hatred of the authentic male. They might not know when to stop hitting.

The light was tricky and the putter made me nervous. If I tried sweet reason, she was going to try to sink it into my skull. So I moved with no regard for chivalry. I feinted toward Bobby, and lunged at Joe. I got a hand on the putter shaft before she could build up any momentum with it. I wrested it out of her hand, reversed it, sidestepped her, and laid the limber end of it across the seat of those khakis. It made a little whirring in the air, and a mighty crack on impact. Joe leaped high and, probably much to her own disgust, gave a high girlish scream of anguish. I turned in time to see Bobby hurl a rock at my head. It tickled the hair on the crown of my head, and the fright lent considerable enthusiasm to my pursuit. Bobby turned in flight. I welted her three hearty times across tight denim, and she joined her yelps to those of her buddy. Joe grappled with me, trying to trip me. She was sobbing in frustration, and she smelled like a mule skinner. I spun her away, and whacked her another beauty. She screamed and gave up and started running toward the trailer.

Bobby made the mistake of running right along beside her, about five feet away from her. I sped into the gap with forehand and backhand. Martha Whippler had come to the doorway to watch them brutalize me. They nearly trampled her in their haste to get out of range. They sounded as if they were trying to yodel. I laughed, hurled the putter well out of the colony, and drove away from there.

Back in the muted silence of the big room at the Apache, Dana slept on. Remembering that the Apache food service would be closed, I had stopped at an implausible delicatessen in town. I turned more lights on. I unsacked my purchases, pried the top off the beef stew with noodles. It was still steaming. I carried it over and sat on the floor beside the bed and wafted it back and forth in front of her face. Her nose twitched, twitched again. Suddenly her eyes opened wide. She focused on me. She gave a great start.

"Hey!" she said. "Hey now!" She gave a great creaking, stretching, shuddering yawn and then reached for the container. She hitched herself up, arranged the pillows, tucked the sheet around her, under her arms, and lifted a huge plastic forkful into the greedy waiting mouth. "Oh!" she said, "Oh my God, Trav, nothing has ever tasted like this."

I moved a small table close to her elbow, brought over the garlic dills, the hot tea and the strawberry cheesecake. I sat on the foot of the bed, admiring her. When the edge of hunger began to be eased, she began to be uncomfortable.

"Did you eat?" she asked.

"Like a wolf."

She poked at her tangled hair. "I'm a mess, I bet "

Her dark vital eyes were puffy, shadowed with fatigue. Her lips were swollen, pale without lipstick. There was a long scratch on her throat, three oval blue smudges on the front of her left shoulder, where my fingers had bruised her.

"You look just fine, Dana."

Her face got pink. She would not look directly at me. "I bet. Uh . . . what time is it?"

"Twenty of one."

She said she would finish the cheesecake later. She asked me to please turn my back. She lugged our suitcase into the bathroom. I heard her take a quick shower. In a little while after the water stopped, she came shyly out, hair brushed, mouth made up, and she was wearing a little blue hip-length nightgown, diaphanous, with lace at throat and hem. Rather than making any attempt to model it, she scuttled for the bed in a knock-kneed half-run, slightly hunched over. She piled in, covered herself and said, blushing furiously, "It isn't exactly what I thought I was buying."

I laughed at her. She frowned part way through the cheesecake and then managed a timid smile, a direct but fleeting glance. "I'm not used to this sort of situation, Trav. I'm sorry."

"Don't be. Nobody else is."

She swallowed and looked pained. "I was so . . . I don't know what you must th . . . . I never . . . Oh *hell*, anyway!"

"Stop fussing. So it's a new relationship. We are something to each other we weren't before. And took a risk. You know that. Somebody, Hemingway maybe, had a definition of a moral act. It's something you feel good after. And, coming back here to you after where I've been makes us seem like the innocence of angels."

She showed her concern. "What happened, dear?"

The cheesecake and tea were long gone by the time I finished with the facts and the speculations.

She looked dubious. "It seems like an *awful* lot of guessing."

I went through it once more, in précis form. "What do we know about M'Gruder? He is feisty, rich, ruthless and stingy. And, with no occupation, he is highly mobile. He's brown and fit and damned callous. Okay, as the purchaser of a service, he got into direct contact with Ives. Ives, seeing a golden opportunity, recognizing Lysa, took all the pictures he could get, hundreds of them, knowing he could crop and enlarge to exhibit every relationship that went on during those four days. Assume that when M'Gruder learned where the party was going to be, he got to a phone and alerted his hired photographer. We know one thing about Ives. He was greedy. He did his job for M'Gruder and got his fee. He collected big from Lysa Dean. He took a hack at the Abbott money and struck out, because Nancy was past protecting.

"Now we have to guess. M'Gruder was hot to marry the young Atlund girl. Her professor father disapproved. M'-

Gruder won him over. I think that with a Swedish girl's traditional respect for parental authority, the professor had to be won over or there would have been no marriage. I think Ives made the mistake of trying to blackmail a previous client, someone who knew who he was and where to find him. The timing fits. Ives threatened to show Professor Atlund the terrace pictures featuring M'Gruder. Anything that rancid would have bitched the marriage forever. The professor would not have his dear girl marrying a libertine like that. Ives did not think M'Gruder dangerous. Maybe he underestimated his stinginess. M'Gruder followed him, saw a good opportunity, and smashed the top of his head in. A couple of weeks later he married his Ulka.

"Take it a step further. We have to assume that Patty M'Gruder learned the name of the photographer from Vance. He would delight in telling her how smart he had been, how cleverly he had cut her loose from the M'Gruder money. He would want to rub her nose in it. He would *have* to hate her. He is a very virile type, and it would be an outrage to his pride to realize his English wife had merely pretended pleasure with him, and actually preferred girls. Patty got a letter from somebody. Gossip, perhaps. Vance's child bride and the problem with the professor. It started her thinking. She had known of Ives' death. She knew Vance. She knew him damned well, and how his mind operated, and his capacity for violence. Somehow, checking this out by phone, she became convinced Vance had done in Ives. So she sent a letter to Vance. It would be a very veiled hint. Come through with the money you cheated me out of, boy, or the Santa Rosita police are going to take an interest in you. Words to that effect. He couldn't risk that. I'd say he'd write back something about planning to be in Phoenix and be willing to discuss her financial situation at that time. She would realize she had struck gold. Now he could not risk being publicly in Las Vegas. When women die, they check out their ex-husbands. I say he set up a good solid alibi in Phoenix, and came over here last night and killed her. He smashed the top of her head in. He would imagine he had no other choice. She hated him as much as he hated her. She would show no mercy. She would bleed him forever."

She thought it over. "I guess it does make sense. But, Trav, is it our problem? Isn't Samuel Bogen our problem, really?"

"At this moment, my darling Dana, some very shrewd cop

may be checking out some small slip M'Gruder made. The death of Patricia *has* to require he be checked out. So they grab him for murder first. Do you think he would maintain a chivalrous silence? He would want to lay all the facts on the line, with little distortions here and there, to try to show justification or at least a plausible excuse for murder. Once they round up Cass and Carl and Martha Whippler and start questioning them one at a time, how long do you think Lysa Dean would stay in the clear. Make up a headline, honey. Star Implicated in Orgy Murder. She'd be even worse off. I have to find out how good these guesses are. If she's going to be in the soup, the best I can do is warn her. Maybe she can take some steps. Long-term contracts. Public relations advice. Something."

Dana frowned. "I see what you mean. But he could have just *said* Phoenix."

"I think he's there. It's close. I want to check it out."

"All right, dear."

I patted her on the foot. "I like obedient women."

She yawned. "I just feel terribly passive, I guess."

"Entirely, completely passive?"

She pursed her lips. She tilted her head. She laid a finger alongside her nose. "Well . . . I wouldn't go so far as to say *that*."

thirteen

I HAD THE RANDOM IDEA of poking around the Four Treys to see if I could find small hint of a visit from Vance M'-Gruder the night of Patty's death, but my few small memories of the hard-nosed vigilance of the Las Vegas cops outweighed the impulse. They deal, day and night, with every kind of spook and hustler in the world, and they would be focused very intently on this murder, and I did not relish the prospect of being bounced up and down while trying to explain my passing interest.

Besides, if M'Gruder was as bright as I imagined, he would not have put in an appearance in the stage lighting of any of the downtown casinos. He would have her Desert Gate address. Once he got to town it would be no great feat to find out when her shift ended. As I shaved I tried to guess his most plausible mode of transportation. It was just about three hundred miles to Phoenix. I decided that if I were doing it, I'd settle for a good fast car. With enough muscle under the hood, and the right kind of springing for the mountain curves, you could safely call it a five-hour run. Leave Phoenix at six and arrive at eleven. Spend an hour hunting her down and killing her. Back by five-thirty in the morning. Sneak into the bridal bed. A private car was safer than a bus, a scheduled flight or a private plane. Cash for gas. No records, no fellow passengers. Properly done, casually done, he could have people convinced he had never left at all. If he had the cold nerve necessary to make that earlier run to Santa Rosita . . .

We walked to the dining room for breakfast, my lady wearing that green which was all she happened to have. My drowsy lady walked close at my side, without haste, her smile as inward and bemused as that of the Mona Lisa. She hugged my arm and beamed up at me and gave me a sleepy wink. And then she yawned.

Between us we ate a mountain of wheat cakes, a bale of bacon.

I found a Phoenix paper in the lobby rack, checked through it and found a society editor by-line. I coached Dana and put her into a phone booth with a fake name and a reasonably plausible cover story. I stood outside the booth and saw her eyes go fierce and bright. She gave me a savage little nod. When she came out, she said, "What a sweet woman! The M'Gruders are staying with a couple named Glenn and Joanne Barnweather. She spake their names with social awe. Old friends of his, apparently. They flew in from Mexico City about five days ago, she thinks. She had an item on it. They're staying at the Barnweather ranch out beyond Scottsdale. You were sure, weren't you?"

"Not completely. But I'm beginning to be. So let's go take a look at them."

We went back to the room and packed. A tremendous chore. She made a housewifely ceremony of it, trotting around the room in a charade of seeing that no meager possession was overlooked, earnest frown between her eyes, white teeth biting into the fullness of underlip.

I caught her as she went by, planted a kiss upon the frown lines and told her that she was a fine girl. She said she was glad I thought she was a fine girl, but it might be a pretty good idea to just leggo of the fine girl or maybe we wouldn't be out of there by noon, which she had happened to notice was checkout time.

We were on our way with the top down heading toward Boulder City by noon, after one quick stop at a department store for a stretch denim skirt and halter top and bright yellow scarf for her, white sport shirt for the driver.

The car was heavy and agile. The day had a honeymoon flavor. The sun and the dry wind baked us. We laughed. We made bad jokes. She slanted dark eyes at me, lively with her mischief. This was the way I had wanted her to be. Totally alive and free, not tucked back into her own darkness.

But, totally alive, she was an impressive handful. This was not some pretty little girl, coyly flirtatious, delicately stimulated. This was the mature female of the species, vivid, handsome and strong, demanding that all the life and need within her be matched. Her instinct would immediately detect any hedging, any dishonesty, any less than complete response to her—and then she would be gone for good. Wholeness was all she could comprehend or accept. For now there were no shadows in her eyes, no hesitations as a bad edge of memory stung her. Even in this pursuit of murder, it was a fine fine world.

When we stopped for lunch in an outdoor patio in heavy shade, I looked at her and said, "Why?"

She knew what I meant. She scowled into her iced coffee. "I guess way back after you came back to the room after seeing Carl Abelle. I don't know. You could have stomped around, the hard-guy grin and all that. But you felt bad about hurting and humiliating him. And he isn't much, certainly. So I figured out you don't go around proving you are a man because you are already sure you are. It isn't all faked up. And in the same way you didn't have to try to use me to prove what a hell of a fellow you are. Even though we were both . . . being attracted in a physical way. I know this sounds as if I'm some kind of an egomaniac, but I just thought well . . . heck, if being a man is a good and valid thing, then there should be like an award of merit or something, an offering. In Abnertalk, namely me. As if I'm so great."

"Don't do that to yourself, Dana. You are implausibly . . . astoundingly, unforgettably great. And I don't mean just in a . . ."

"I know. It isn't me, and it isn't you. Let's not talk about it. It's the total of us, the crazy total. I'm not going to talk about it, or think of what comes after. Okay? Okay, darling?"

"No talk. No analysis."

"We are kind of beautiful," she said. "It's enough to know that, I guess. Alone I'm just . . . sort of efficient and severe and a little heavy-handed. Defensive. Alone you're just sort of a rough, wry opportunist, a little bit cold and shrewd and watchful. Cruel, maybe. You and your sybarite boat and your damned beach girls. But we add up to beautiful in some crazy way. For now."

"For now, Dana?"

"I'm no kid, Travis. I know hurt is inevitable always."

"Shut up."

"I talk too much?"

"Only sometimes."

So off we went, to Kingman, to Wikieup, to Congress—up into cold places, down into heats—to Wickenburg, to Wittman, and down into the richness of the old Salt River Valley where Phoenix presides over the boom that threatens never to quit. It has become a big fast rough grasping town, where both the irrigation heiresses and the B girls wear the same brand of ranch pants.

The sun was low behind us as we came in, breasting the outgoing traffic of the close of Friday business. I cruised and settled for a glassy sprawl called The Hallmark, a big U of stone, teak and thermo-windows enclosing a great green of lawn and gardens, a blue of water in a marbled pool in the shape of a painter's pallette. In a nearby specialty shop, still open, we let Lysa Dean refurbish our dwindled wardrobes to the extent of swim trunks for me and a swim suit for the lady. We fixed ourselves tall ones of gin and bitter lemon. Dana swam with utmost earnestness, chin held very high, using a stroke I told her was early sheep dog. In the bathroom, in fading light of day, her body bore the halter marks of the long sunny ride, her broad flat breasts pale, responsive to soapy ablutions cooperatively offered. In a predictable haste, I toted the untoweled seal-shape of her, dripping, to bed, a firm, lithe, gleaming, chuckling burden which seemed to have no weight at all. Ceremonial celebration of our twenty-fourth hour.

Eased and complete, in mild and affectionate embrace, we took up the duty of talking about M'Gruder, weighing the merits of the possible methods of contact.

I could not tell her precisely what I hoped to accomplish. If M'Gruder was the man, I wanted to stir him up. I didn't want him to believe he had any chance at all. A man running is a dead man. A trial would finish Lysa Dean as well. And when you take someone's money for expenses, there is a morality involved. He would have some confidence he had gotten away with it. I had to blast that out of him and set him running. And arrange a chase.

The Barnweather number was listed. We went over it carefully. I coached her. She added a few ideas. There was a phone extension in the bath. I went in there and listened.

A servant said the M'Gruders were in the guest house. He gave Dana another number to call.

A man answered. A cultivated baritone, loosened slightly by drink, admitting that he, indeed, was Mister M'Gruder himself.

"You don't know me, Mr. M'Gruder."

"From your charming voice, that is my loss, my dear. What is your name?"

"I've just picked a new name for myself. I wondered if you'd like it. Patty Ives. Do you like that name?"

It was a slow five-count before he spoke. His voice was under careful control. "You sound as if you thought you were telling me something. But I am afraid I don't follow."

"I guess I do have you at a disadvantage. I know so *much* more about you than you know about me."

"I don't wish to be rude, but I don't like guessing games, whoever you are. So if you don't mind . . ."

"I thought we might make a date for a quiet talk, if you would like to sneak away from your little bride, Vance. We have mutual friends. Carl Abelle. Lysa Dean. Cass Edgars. Nancy Abbott. Martha Whippler. Of course Sonny Catton is dead. Poor Sonny."

Again I could have counted to five. "I think you might be a very foolish girl."

"Foolish, but not very greedy. And very, very careful, Vance."

"Let me put it this way. You might have something you think is valuable. But suppose it is only an annoyance?"

"Oh, wouldn't it have to be a *lot* more than that!"

"You are talking in circles, my dear. I am quite certain I can be forgiven for old indiscretions. Life with my ex often became very unwholesome. Mrs. M'Gruder is aware of that. I've reformed. The police were here yesterday afternoon, cooperating with the Las Vegas police, I imagine. To make certain I hadn't killed Patty. I'm not sorry she's dead. I'm not that much of a hypocrite. She was a horrid woman. I had to get free of her in any way I could. All this is none of your business, of course. But I didn't want you to think you've alarmed me. You just make me feel . . . irritable. Please don't phone me again." Click.

I reached and put the phone on the hook and then sat back on the wide yellow rim of the little triangular tub. In a few moments Dana appeared in the bathroom doorway. She had put on my sport shirt. She leaned against the door frame and said, "Well?"

"I don't know. I just don't know. Either we're dead wrong, or he's got the nerve of a headwaiter. So much points his way. Damn it, it *has* to be him. We're going out there."

"Just like that?"

"We're going to be invited out, I hope."

There is one theory that there are but a hundred thousand people in the United States, and the rest of the 189,900,000 is a faceless mob. The theory further states that any person in the hundred thousand can be linked to any other by no more than a three-step process. Example: Ron knew Carol's brother at Princeton; Carol's husband worked with Vern at the Ford Foundation; Vern's cousin met Lucy at the film festival. Thus when Ron and Lucy meet as strangers, and sense that they are each members of the hundred thousand, they can play a warm and heartening and satisfying game of who-do-you-know, and, with little cries of delight, trace the relationship.

By dint of past endeavors I had acquired provisional membership in the group, and it seemed likely to me that Glenn and Joanne Barnweather would be solid members. So I had to tap other members most likely to know them. I tried Tulio in Oklahoma City and drew a dead blank. I remembered Mary West in Tucson. She knew them, but not well. But she did know Paul and Betty Diver in Flagstaff who knew them intimately, and she was certain she could get Betty to play along. If there was any hitch, she would phone back. If not, I would hear from Joanne Barnweather directly. She briefed me on what I'd have to know about the Divers.

We had a twenty-minute wait before the phone rang. "Trav McGee?" a woman asked. "This is Joanne Barnweather. I just got a call from our very dear mutual friend, Paul Diver, saying you're in town. Could you come out to the place? Are you free?"

"If I can bring along a gal."

"Of *course* you can, dear. Glenn and I will be delighted. We've got some people in to meet our houseguests and we're just churning around here, very informal, drinking up a small storm and waiting for time to throw a steak on. Do come as you are. We'll be delighted to see you." She gave me directions.

Dana had been nestled close to me, listening. When I hung

up she gave me a look of mock admiration. "You are a scoundrel, McGee."

"Darling, go put on your green."

"She said to come as we are."

"Then at least button my shirt."

fourteen

ON THE WAY out, under a chilly spangle of stars, I had briefed Dana on how we'd handle it. She was to stay away from M'Gruder, target on his young Swede bride if possible. I would do what I could with M'Gruder.

The Barnweather place was a simple little quarter-million-dollar ranch house a few hundred yards into a lot of rocky acreage, with fifteen cars glinting in the starlight, music and festive sounds coming from the floodlighted pool area.

I sensed that Dana took a deep breath and braced herself as we walked toward the party jabber. There were infrared heaters focused on the broad terrace area at the house end of the pool. A gleaming, beaming little fellow in a red coat tended bar. These were a pack of the young marrieds, the success-prone ones. The tense and girlish mothers of three and five and seven young, their beefier husbands, expansive with bourbon and land deals. About thirty-five people in all, forming and reforming their little conversational groups. Dress was varied, all the way from shorts and slacks to some of those fanciful ranch coats on the men, the pale whipcord jobs with the pearl buttons and pocket flaps. The audible talk had that Southwest flavor so quickly acquired by the people who move there from Indiana and Pennsylvania.

When we hesitated, a slender pretty woman came smiling toward us, holding one hand out to each of us. "Trav? I'm Joanne."

"And this is Diana Hollis." We had decided it was possible Lysa Dean had spoken of her girl Friday to M'Gruder, and the name was just unusual enough to stick in his mind.

135

"So glad you could come, dears. Come meet the group."

She steered us over for a drink first, and then swung us through the throng, rattling off the names and identifications. Glenn was one of the burly ones in whipcord. Joanne made a little more special thing of the introduction to their house guests. Vance M'Gruder was a little balder, a little browner, a little taller than he had seemed in the pictures. He was a type. The totally muscled sportsman—muscles upon muscles so that even his face looked like a leather bag of walnuts. Polo muscles, tennis muscles, sail-handling muscles, fencing muscles—the type who does handstands every morning of his life, works out with professionals whenever possible, and has a savage and singleminded desire to whip you at anything you're willing to play with him, from squash racquets to tetherball. He had the personality to go with the body—a flavor of remote, knowing, arrogant amusement.

His young bride was one of the most striking females I have ever seen in my life. You had a tendency to speak to her in a hushed voice, an awed voice. The Swedes grow some of the finest specimens of our times. This Ulka Atlund M'Gruder was big enough for M'Gruder to keep her in flat heels at all times. She wore a woolly tangerine-colored shift. Her arms were bare. The others were bundled in jackets, sweaters, tunics, shawls, stoles. She looked as if she had enough animal heat to keep her entirely comfortable at thirty below. Her body, under the touch of the fabric, was ripe, leggy and entirely perfect. Without makeup, her features were almost those of some heroic, dedicated young boy, a page from the time of King Arthur. Or an idealized Joan of Arc. Her tilted gray-green-blue Icelandic eyes were the cold of northern seas. Her hair was a rich, ripe, heavy spill of pale pale gold, curved across the high and placid brow. She had little to say, and a sleepy and disinterested way of saying it. Her eyes kept seeking out her husband. Over all that stalwart Viking loveliness there was such a haze of sensuality it was perceptible, like a strange matte finish. It was stamped into the slow and heavy curve of her smile, marked by the delicate violet shadows under her eyes, expressed by the cant of her high round hips in the way she stood. Though by far the youngest person there, she at the same time seemed far older. She had been bolted to the bowsprit of an ancient ship for a thousand years. And every woman there hated her and feared her. The look of her confirmed my guesses about Vance M'Gruder. Wearing this one like a banner or a medal was the ultimate cachet of competitive masculinity. She had a strange primitive flavor of sexual docility. She was indentured to M'Gruder, totally focused upon him, yet were she taken from him by someone with more strength and force and purpose, she would shift loyalty without question or hesitation. A man like M'Gruder would go to any length to acquire her. And he had. I was certain of that. I thought of M'Gruder's past habits and inclinations, and I wondered if, when his physical resources began to flag he would stimulate himself by corrupting her. A woman to him would be something owned, to use as he wished.

Later, standing in a group with M'Gruder, I looked over and saw Dana alone with Ulka, talking quietly to her. Ulka nodded. She was watching Vance. I could not get anywhere with Vance. I tried to play do-you-know with him, bringing up the names of some of the Florida sailboat bums I know. Yes, he knew them. Sure. So what. I guessed he could not become interested in trivia. He had taken two horrible risks to acquire and keep the Viking princess. Maybe somebody was getting set to drop the noose on him and end it. Apprehension could make small talk almost impossible. I could not comprehend M'Gruder's promise to put this creature back into college. I found it hard to believe that a professorial type had spawned her. In days of old whenever one of these rarities appeared, one of the king's agents would run to the castle with the news, and the girl-child would disappear forever into one of the royal suites, and her family would get a little sack of gold coins in exchange. In these more random times they are grabbed off by oil men, celebrity athletes, television moguls and M'Gruders. But the man who has one stays nervous because, unless you are a king, you don't really get to own it. It is on temporary loan from providence.

Later I sat near Ulka in a big game room in the house while she carved and chewed her way through a huge rare steak, knife and teeth flashing, jaw muscles and throat working, her eyes made blank by a total concentration on this physical gratification. The effort made a sweaty highlight on her pale brow, and at last she picked up the sirloin bone and gnawed it bare, putting a slick of grease on lips and fingertips. There was no vulgarity in this hunger, any more than when a tiger cracks the hip socket to suck the marrow.

The party fragmented, and there was room enough for them to roam all the house and grounds, various degrees of alcohol dividing them more positively than social class or business interest. I had lost track of Dana, and I went night-walking in unhurried search. Skirting a tall cactus garden, floodlighted in eerie blue, I heard, off to my right, a conspiratorial rasp of female venom. "Bastard! Bastard! Bastard!" It was more contemptuous than indignant. I sought to move quietly out of range. I did not care how husbands were gutted in this desert paradise. I imagined it was done the same as elsewhere.

But the male voice stopped me. "All I want to know is where you . . ." The rest of the sentence was lost. He had raised his voice to cut her off and lowered it as she fell silent. But it was Vance M'Gruder.

"You are so smart! You are *soooooo* smart! Oh, *God*, what a brilliant mind I married!"

"Sssh, Ullie. Don't shout!"

"Maybe it was one of my Mexican boyfriends. How about that? Hah? How about that? And just what would you do about it?" Sweet voice of Ulka Atlund M'Gruder, bride of two months. And where was the sleepy remote smile? The placid acceptance? This was the malignancy of a taunting woman, an emasculating woman. He shushed her again and they moved off, out of range. I circled and discovered I had been near the path that probably led over to the guest house.

I admit feeling a certain dirty little satisfaction. It was as if the fox had made one leap just high enough and found out the grapes actually *were* sour. Here was this brown hard bundle of sport muscles trying to kid the calendar by wedding the glorious child bride, and now all his game-skills and all his money and his social standing were no defense at all against that killer-instinct which could launch her right at his most vulnerable point, his aging masculinity. Seeking paradise, he had embraced a sweet disaster.

The party dwindled. Laughter was drunken. A group sang "The Yellow Rose of Texas."

I stood with Dana, saying goodnight, and Joanne Barn-weather swayed against us, and said, "You all come riding tomorrow morning, you hear? Got lovely horses. Jus' lovely. Diana, sweetie, like I said, I got stuff'll fit you. Don' worry 'bout it. Jus' you all and us and the M'Gruders. You know what, Diana? Ulka liked you. She wants you 'long. How about that anyhow? To find out she likes anybody. Crissake, we've known Vance forever and we love the sweet ol' son of a bitch, and it was great he got loose from that limey dyke, believe me, but hones' I can't figure this Ulka. Sheese! A zombie, thass what she is. I shouldn't talk like this, but I'm a wee little bit stoned, sweeties. What you do, you get here like nine in the morning, okay?"

On the way home Dana said, "Horses scare me."

"How did you make out?"

"Didn't you hear? She likes me. But I never would have been able to tell. Trav, that child has very limited reactions, really. I had a friend who got like that once. They said finally it was a hypothyroid condition. She sort of drifted, slept fourteen hours a night and couldn't keep track of conversations. Believe me, dear, I tried. I really tried. I had about forty minutes alone with her. I tried to drop key words into it to get some kind of a reaction. After a long struggle I did find out that her husband played poker last Wednesday night. He loves a good poker session, she said. She said he didn't come back until Thursday just before noon. I practically had to shake her to get that much out of her."

I did not tell Dana I felt uneasy. I had the feeling the play was being taken away from us. I had made a move. Now either this was all in innocence, or M'Gruder was making one. I resolved to handle myself as though he were making a move. Violence is the stepchild of desperation.

We both had to borrow gear. Glenn Barnweather's pants were too short in the leg and big in the waist for me. Dana had a slightly different problem with Joanne's twill britches. The waist was fine and the length was good, but in thigh and bottom Dana filled them to bursting. The stable hands saddled the mounts while a rather shaky Joanne doled out therapeutic rum sours. Joanne assigned the mounts. Dana, as a novice, got a rather plump and amiable mare. I was given a hammerhead buckskin with a rolling eye. He sensed a certain incompetence and tried to simultaneously nibble my leg and bash me into a post. I sawed him and kicked him into a dubious docility. By all odds, as we went clattering and snorting up a long baked slope, Joanne and Vance were the best of the group. Elbows in, heels correct, moving like a part of the animal. Glenn on a big red stallion was a close second. Ulka and I were about on a level. She looked glorious in pale blue denim with a white cowgirl hat on the back of her fair head, laced under her chin. Ulka seemed much merrier than on the night before. But Vance looked wretched. He had a greenish look under his tan. His eyes were bloodshot. With the air of a man under great tension he had knocked down three sours in rapid order before mounting.

Joanne chattered about the ranch and what they were eventually going to do with it. She pointed out where things would be. My damned horse kept trying to stumble to see if he could loosen me a little bit, then hurl me the rest of the way. For a time I rode beside Ulka. She dipped into a pale leather pouchpurse she wore looped around one wrist and got out cigarettes, leaned and gave me one, then leaned and after several near-misses, managed to give me a light. We smiled in wordless idiocy at each other. Her big breasts bounced very firmly under the denim. Her classic nose was shiny. I lost her when my horse moved up from a canter into a full run. He didn't seem to like a canter. He tended to drop back into a spine-shattering trot, or suddenly go like hell. He kept me busy. Suddenly everybody, at Glenn's suggestion, went careering across rocky flats toward a distant stand of trees. My horse was beginning to take me a little more seriously. We were spread out. Dana was up with Glenn, hunched toward the horse's neck, perhaps grasping at the saddle horn, pale pants bouncing. Joanne was at my left and a half a length ahead of me.

That was when Ulka Atlund M'Gruder gave her terrible, piercing scream. The horses had violent reactions. I went up with mine and came down with mine, then spurred him forward and caught at Dana just as she began to slip off the side of her mare's neck, hauled her back toward the saddle. Glenn had taken off to the left. I looked and saw M'Gruder's horse running wildly in that direction, with a terrible ragdoll figure bounding along the rocks beside the rear hooves. It slipped free and lay still, wet-shiny with some patches of red. Ulka dismounted and, screaming again, ran stumbling across the rocks to drop beside the figure. I dropped off and knotted my barbarous steed to a dwarfed bush. Dana's mare suddenly took off, heading for home. Joanne reined around and set out after Dana. I ran over to the body. It took one look to identify it forever as such. I pulled Ulka to her feet and walked her away from it. She was shuddering, over and over.

"He just leaned forward and slipped off," she said in her thin little voice with just a trace of accent. "He slipped off but his foot was caught. He just leaned forward and slipped off. Oh my God." She dropped onto her knees and haunches, face in her hands.

They brought the body back in a jeep and transferred it into an ambulance near the Barnweather house. The necessary red tape was handled with dispatch. We all agreed that M'Gruder had not seemed well. Ulka said that he'd had a stomach upset and had not slept. She rested in Joanne's bedroom. Joanne and Dana were with her. Her father was notified. He would arrive in Phoenix Sunday morning to take her back to San Francisco. The funeral would be there. M'Gruder's lawyer was notified. Reporters hovered around, sitting in cars, looking irritable.

I sat in the terrace shade with Glenn Barnweather. He kept shaking his head and saying, "Hell of a thing, hell of a thing," and then fixing himself another stiff bourbon.

"He certainly had everything to live for," I said.

"Christ, you ought to see his place in Hawaii. Her place now, I guess. You know why it hits her so damned hard having it happen right now? I got woozy last night. If I'd gone to bed, I'd have been sick. I took a little walk. Sounds carry in the night. They were having one hell of a battle last night. Screaming at each other. I couldn't hear the words. It went on a long time. You wouldn't think she could get that worked up, would you? Maybe it was their first fight. I had the idea he was in charge. Maybe he thought so too. A man married two months and he can stay out all night for poker when there's that item home in bed, you *know* he has to be boss."

"Poker?"

"Down in town at the club last Wednesday. It's a regular thing. All-night session once a month. He dropped about two thousand. I got some of it. I would have had more, but he came back pretty good toward the end."

When you sell yourself something, and all the parts fit, you resent the hell out of having somebody kick the foundation out from under it. You want to grab the structure to keep it from falling down.

"He played all night long?" I said, looking at that big red earnest face, looking in vain for any hint of lie or evasion.

His fleeting grin was mildly lewd. "Well into the bright cruel light of day, McGee. I can understand anybody being startled, after a good look at that Swede bride. Maybe poor Vance had to take a breather. She looks like one hell of a project."

My pretty tower fell down. Fallacious suppositions make a hell of a jangle when they hit the dirt, particularly when you dislike the person you've nominated. I'd heard one little piece of that quarrel too, a piece that could be related to the previous Wednesday night. Maybe I'd heard him asking her where she'd gone that night. And she taunted him about Mexican boyfriends . . .

"Did Ulka have a night on the town too?" I asked him.

"She was going to, but not what you'd call a real swinging situation. One of Joanne's concert things. I miss every one I can. Cocktails and a dinner party and a concert party. It was all set up, and Ulka decided not to go, and Joanne went alone."

"Maybe Ulka went out later. Did they have a rental car?"

"I loaned them the Corvette I bought Jo. It's the three-sixty, and it's just too much car for her. It scares her. Vance was wondering about buying it and they could drive it to San Francisco and have the rest of their stuff shipped. Okay with me, but we didn't get around to making the deal. It's new. About fifteen hundred miles on it. It scares Jo. She gets absent-minded and gooses it and it scares her."

"Was that Wednesday night the only time they've been apart?"

"He stuck pretty close to her."

"They drive around in that car much?"

"We were keeping them too busy. What's this all about?"

I shrugged. "Nothing. Idle chatter." After some small talk, he fixed himself another drink and ambled off into the house. I went down the path to the guest house. The Sting Ray was in the carport, top down. I looked at the speedometer, and then walked slowly and thoughtfully back to the main house. I couldn't tell Glenn what was on my mind. The toppled pieces of my theory suddenly looked good again. I was putting it back together, with a new name on it. The problem was motive. A weird guess stopped me in my tracks. I took long strides the rest of the way to the main house.

I whispered to Dana in the hallway. "Honey, just keep anybody from going into that bedroom. Make any excuse you can think of."

"You look so strange, darling."

"I feel strange."

"Can you tell me?"

"When I'm sure. Then I can tell you."

I went into Joanne's bedroom and closed the door behind me. It was a long room. The draperies were drawn. It was early afternoon. Ulka reclined on a quilted yellow chaise with a fuzzy yellow blanket over her lap. Her slanted eyes were reddened. She was still in her stretch denim, and drifting on the airconditioned chill was the faint effluvium of saddle horse. She watched me with apparent unconcern as, without greeting, I pulled a hassock over close to the chaise and sat facing her. She had so much presence I had to remind myself she was, after all, just an eighteen-year-old girl, with the very last diminishing hint of a childish roundness in her cheeks.

Silence is a useful gambit, but I could not tell if it was having any effect at all upon her.

"Well, Ullie," I said.

"I will never let anyone else ever call me that, all my life."

"That's very sentimental, Ullie. Very tender-hearted. I guess you are a very tender-hearted girl. You didn't want your father upset, did you? Those pictures Ives took of your husband-to-be would have upset the professor. He would have forbidden the marriage. And you are a dutiful daughter. Ives was a very greedy fellow. He knew how badly Vance wanted you. He must have asked for a great deal of money. You know, it wasn't smart of Ives to blackmail his previous client with the pictures he took, because Vance knew him. Ives must have decided Vance was incapable of violence."

She frowned and shook her pretty head. "Ives? Pictures? Blackmail? Why do you come in here with this crazy talk?"

"Ives had to get it in one big chunk because as soon as you were married to Vance, there was no more leverage Ives could use. I guess Vance must have confessed the problem to you and showed you the pictures, perhaps to see if you would marry without Daddy's permission, so he could save a bundle. It's pretty sad and funny, Ullie. Your great respect for your father, and no respect for life."

"You should not call me Ullie. I will not permit it."

"Vance must have thought it was just a marvelous accident when Ives got killed. All he cared was that it got him off the hook, and when no confederate appeared to pick up where Ives had left off, he knew he was home free. He was going to have the girl, the gold ring and everything. His tragedy was in slowly finding out what a psychotic bitch you really are."

"Who are you? You must be mad, entirely."

"Let's check it out together, Ullie. No one suspected Vance. Patty, his ex-wife, was the only one in the world in a position to brood about it and begin to add two and two. And finally she got an answer and checked it out as closely as she could, and knew she had Vance right where she wanted him. She had every reason to want to get back at him. Believing Vance had killed Ives, and knowing that he could be a good big source of income to her for the rest of her life, she got in touch with him. I think we can figure out how that went wrong, Ullie. Vance could prove where he was on the night of December fifth. But where was his darling girl? Quite a husky girl. And someone who could get close to Ives and close to Patty at night, in lonely places, whereas Vance couldn't have managed it. After you'd bashed Ives, Patty was a necessity. Clumsy murder is like housework, dear. Once you begin, you're never really finished."

"All this is so absurd, and so boring."

"Patty would have persisted, and sooner or later Vance would have had to face the idea that you killed Ives. Maybe he couldn't stomach that. Maybe he would have turned you in. He was finding out that his marriage wasn't what he had counted on."

"We couldn't have been happier!"

"Ullie! Ullie! What about the Mexican boyfriends? Just little flirtations, I imagine. Just enough to keep him off balance, make him sweat."

"How could you. . . ." She stopped. I could guess she remembered how he had tried to shush her. Her breathing had gone slightly shallow and there were spots of color in flawless cheeks. I saw her recover herself with an effort, slowing and deepening her breathing.

"I don't imagine Vance really wanted to play poker. You left unobserved, you got back unobserved. Home free. But all it would take would be legwork, Ullie. One of those plodding methodical checks of every gas station along the way.

You didn't have the range. Some little joker is probably still dreaming about you—the most beautiful girl he ever saw, coming in out of the night in that Sting Ray."

"So? I got very restless. I took a drive. I drive very fast. Can I help it if Vance got very suspicious of me, if he got very foolish ideas? You don't know how it is . . . how it was. He wanted to be . . . so very young and lively and fun, to be like boys I know. But really he wanted things quieter. I could see strangers laughing at him. He should have had *dignity*! Certainly I wanted all that money and travel and clothes and fun. A professor has a shabby little life. All my life I knew the husband I would have, older and very rich and strong, to buy me everything and adore me, to sit and smile at me and admire me when I danced with all the young men, and trust me. When I'd found him I could not lose him. But every day was a contest to see . . . which one of us was younger. He did not understand how love should be a perfection. All he cared was how many times he could take me. He thought that was another way to be young. Why did he have to prove so much? I can tell about you. You would understand. You are older too, but not as old as he was. You are stronger, Travis McGee. There is the money now. I listened when you told Joanne about your funny little boat with the funny name." She closed her eyes for a moment, opened them wide and looked at me. "You see, I have always . . . felt like a special person. As if my life would be . . . beautiful and important. Things happen in strange ways. Vance was not the one. But suddenly you are here. It is strange. It is so strange the way we both have that little feeling it would be . . . what was planned for us all along."

It was such a fabulous con job, I could feel the dirty dreams seeping into my mind. Help her cover up the mistakes she'd made. That was the unspoken offer. And you get the girl on a platter. Mmmm . . . trade the *Busted Flush* for a really good motor sailer, crew of three—captain, steward, deck hand—and see how many sheltered coves in the world's oceans had really top-grade moonlight. And, of course, remember never to turn your back to her . . .

"Ullie, dear, we can't get onto a new subject until we finish the first one. I repeat your interesting statement. 'When I found him I could not lose him.' But he finally worked himself into a position where you had to lose him. I knew he was prying at you to find out where you'd gone, and I wondered why he thought you'd gone anywhere. Then Glenn told me about Vance thinking he might buy the car. Men who think of buying cars kick the tires and slam the doors and check the mileage. So he checked the mileage, and then he checked it again and found a great big inexplicable addition, taking it up to past two thousand. He hadn't put it on, so you had, and Patty was dead in the same way Ives was dead, and he found himself in a pretty eerie marriage. I'll make a little guess, Ullie. From the way he acted this morning, I don't think he got much sleep. I think he kept digging at you until you opened up and told him the whole thing. Then after you told him, you realized he couldn't exactly forgive and forget. He couldn't handle it. It was too much. Maybe he felt so wretched he didn't want to take any morning ride, but you knew that sooner or later you could maneuver it so that all the rest of us would be ahead of you two."

"Could I be such a monster, darling? Could you believe that of me, really?"

That narrow leather pouchpurse was in the chaise beside her hip. She made a futile grab for it as I took it quickly. It was new. I examined it and found a little area still moist near the bottom seam. The leather thongs were long and sturdy. Holding it by the thongs, I felt the deadly heft and balance of it. It was like a sock with a rock in the toe. It was a skull smasher, wicked as a medieval flail. I opened the pouch top, reached in and fumbled past lipstick, little comb, cigarettes and matches, and pulled out a rabbit. It was carved of some dense gray stone, sitting hunched, ears laid back, crude, a lump about two-thirds the size of a baseball.

"There is the leg work with the gas stations, and there are the miracles of modern chemistry, Ullie. The tiny little blotch of blood on this, with maybe a sweet little tuft of hubby's hair stuck thereon, scrubbed off nicely right there in Joanne's bathroom. But a police lab can prove it was human blood hereon, though they can't type it. And they can dismantle the plumbing and find traces in the drain in there. I imagine that after Ives and Patty you disposed of the bags. They'd have been a lot messier."

"That's a very old bunny," she said. "It's primitive folk art from Iceland."

"Ullie, a good enough lawyer might be able to plead you sick and buy the experts to back him up. Age would be a consideration, of course. And beauty. Maybe you are sick. I don't know. Perhaps it is just an egoism so intense other people don't seem quite real to you. Murder wouldn't seem real then either, I suppose."

She tilted her head. "Vance cried and cried. He hugged me and said he would get me the best. . . ." She stopped, gnawed her thumb knuckle, looked at me in a speculative way. The admission had been made, and I could not tell if it was inadvertent, or meant to look inadvertent. "You can understand, Travis. There's such a thing as thinking of the best for everybody concerned. I'd very much like to have you take me home to Father. I know you would like each other, very much. He is very old-fashioned, you know. He would want me to wait a year. Waiting isn't too hard, is it, when you're sure?"

I bounced the bunny in the palm of my hand, dropped it back into the lethal sack, yanked the drawstring tight. I could not even tell if she knew what a desperate game she was playing. She sat up, reached and closed her warm strong hand around my wrist. I was planning the words to tell her I was blowing the whistle when I heard the door behind me open slowly. I realized, as I turned, I had spent a long time with the bereaved widow, and Dana might be having problems keeping people out.

Dana stared in at us from the doorway. "Joanne has to . . ."

"I'm through here, honey," I said. "Tell Glenn to phone the law. This eerie child killed all three of them, and she made so many mistakes it won't be hard to . . ."

I had made the elementary mistake of taking my eyes off Ulka. When the pouch bag was ripped out of my hand, I did not bother to turn around and see what she was going to do with it. I dived to my left, away from the chaise, but bunny-rabbit still glanced off my skull and came down onto my shoulder, smashing the collarbone. I sprawled on the floor, with my ears roaring and with lights spangling my vision, absolutely unable to avoid a second and mortal crunching if she had taken time. But a vagueness moved past me with tiger pace, and I made a stifled whimper which was supposed to be a roar of warning to Dana. As vision cleared, as I got onto my knees, I saw Dana go down flat and heavy and hopelessly limp, onto her face. I heard a distant shout of query and alarm. I began the slow crawl toward my woman.

fifteen

I HAD A PRETTY FAIR CONCUSSION, just enough so that I had blackouts, and they kept shining lights into my eyes, testing my reflexes, and giving me mental arithmetic to solve. My right arm, taped across my chest, felt leaden, and the smashed bone caused enough pain to keep them sticking needles into me. It made me groggy, and I kept asking about Dana. Miss Holtzer is in surgery. Miss Holtzer is still in surgery. Miss Holtzer is in the recovery room.

Then it was Sunday morning and I was told that Miss Holtzer was doing as well as could be expected. It is a dim phrase. Who sets up the expectations?

Glenn Barnweather arrived with a big solemn face, a hundred sighs, a sad shaking of the head, a rich smell of bourbon to tell me Ulka was dead. I already knew that, but I didn't know how.

"She took off in the Corvette, northeast out 65 like a goddam road race, and they still can't figure how she got past as many curves as she did. They put a roadblock up there in the straight, way beyond Sunflower, one car blocking the road, and she came down on it at, they estimate, a hundred and thirty or better. Tried to cut around it. Hit the gravel, skidded, hit a rock, went two hundred and fifty feet through the air, hit and bounced and went over a rim and down a thousand-foot slope, bouncing all the way, and the final couple of hundred feet on fire. Like you told the cops, McGee, she must have been crazed with grief. That's right, isn't it? Crazed with grief."

"Out of her head completely. Maniacal strength. You've heard of that."

"I've heard of that. And Diana Hollis turns into Dana Holtzer. What goes on, old buddy?"

"We have to try to protect a lady's reputation, don't we?"

"Oh, sure. Hell, what you do is your own business, I guess, but Jo is going to come in here and really blow her stack."

"I guess she checked with the Divers."

"And Mary West, who wouldn't tell her a damned thing. So she's steaming."

"Glenn, how about you finding out just how Dana is. I would appreciate it very much."

"Glad to do anything for an old buddy who tells me every little thing," he said. He came back in a half hour. "She's one sick gal, Trav. They spent six hours picking little bits of bone out of the front of her brain, right here. And I find out she works for Lysa Dean. That's going to intrigue hell out of Jo. They say Dana's going to be okay." He stood up. "You'll be able to see her by tomorrow."

More officials visited me. I told my tale of hysterical violence again, the young bride crazed by her terrible loss.

Joanne came in. She was furious. After fifteen minutes she was merely resentful, reluctantly accepting the fact there must be some good reason why she'd never find out all she wanted to know. She was decent enough to do some errands for me, like telling The Hallmark to save the room for me, like getting a phone put in, like getting a resident neurosurgeon to come in and give me some straight answers on Dana. He said she should take two months' rest and recuperation before going back to work. I had passed my tests and would be released Monday, unless I acquired some new symptoms. He said not to worry about how she'd act on Monday when I could see her for a few minutes. She would be dazed and semi-conscious still, and might not know me.

After he left I was planning to try to locate Lysa Dean, but she phoned me, putting one very nervous quaver in the switchboard operator's voice. Lysa was terribly dramatic and terribly concerned about everything, full of elaborate reassurances about hospital bills—but shrewd enough to play the whole thing as though I was Dana's dear friend who had accompanied her on her little vacation. She said she and her whole entourage would stop off on the way back to the

Coast, but she couldn't be sure exactly when they could manage it.

On Monday I got dressed and paid my bill and had five minutes with Dana. She was in an adhesive turban, face bloated, shiny, streaked with bruise marks, slits revealing dazed eyes, mouth cracked and puffy. She seemed to know me. She squeezed my hand. I could not understand her mumblings. The nurse stood by and called time on me and sent me away. I moved back into The Hallmark. On Tuesday I saw her three times, morning, afternoon, evening, ten minutes each time. She knew me, and her diction was better, but she was unaware of what had happened to her and seemed in no hurry to find out. She had a tendency to drop off and start snoring in the middle of a vague remark, but she did like her hand held.

At midnight on Tuesday I was awakened by a phone call from an abjectly apologetic fellow telling me that Lysa Dean was in residence at the best hotel in town, and wanted to see me right away. I told him to tell Lysa Dean to go emote up a rope and hung up. I picked up my phone and told The Hallmark switchboard to leave me in peace until nine the next morning. The pinned bone made dressing too much of a problem. If she wanted me, she knew where I was.

Just as I got back to sleep, forty minutes later, there was a brisk knock at my door. Muttering various Anglo-Saxon expressions, I got up and adjusted my sling and went in my shorts to the door. A portly chap in a black suit entered, followed by a Hallmark porter carrying the luggage which Dana and I had checked on to New York and couldn't retrieve in time.

"I'm Herm Louker," he said with an air of imparting information any fool would know. When I looked blank he said, "From the agency." It was supposed to explain everything.

He dipped two fingers into a breast pocket, pulled out two crisp dollars, crackled them very loudly as he handed them to the porter.

Herm looked somewhat like a penguin. He had the same walk. He wore a hairpiece, with a deep wave. His eyes were cigar holes in a hotel towel. He had gold jewelry. He settled himself into a chair, sliced the end off a cigar with a gold knife, lit it with a gold lighter.

"Let me make myself entirely clear, Mr. McGee. The client's interest is my interest. Aside from loving that little woman personally, because she is all doll, through and through, what I got in my mind is a maximum protection of her interests and mine and the industry's." He held up a fat warning hand. "In addition to that, before we go further, I've got also a nervous stomach, and I want to know no more than I already know. I have been with her in Miami, New York and Chicago, and she was a great little trouper, performing in every way. They love that girl all over America. She is all star."

"So I'd better know how much you know."

"Merely that there has been, we shall say, an indiscretion. Show business people, Mr. McGee, are high-spirited and hot-blooded, and some people can take advantage. What we have going is an unfortunate situation where some character wants to give her a rough time. What the little lady feels is that after you started to perform, then you went off on a tangent. Time has been wasted. We got certain information from you in New York. One Samuel Bogen wanted already by the cops. There is no picture. Fingerprints only. A complete description which could be ninety-five thousand guys including me, almost. So we laid on special guards with that description in mind. Nothing in New York. Nothing in Chicago. No contact. As I get it, certain financial inducements were offered. Our star gets nervous, Mr. McGee. What we need now is some way to bring this to a head. If you can solve that, the little lady says she will live up to her end of your deal. I do not want to know your deal, believe me."

"I had one idea worked out."

"So?"

"I wanted to be part of it. I'm not in top shape at the moment."

"So I see."

"It depends on several things. Could you set up a time for her arrival at Los Angeles by air and give it a lot of publicity around Los Angeles?"

"But naturally. It's done every day."

"The man who is after her is disturbed. I think that except for one trip to Vegas, he's stayed in the Los Angeles area. He might come to the airport. He might be waiting at her house. He may want money. He may want to kill her. He might not even know which he wants."

"Please. It gives me cramps."

"You have to know a few things, Mr. Louker. We don't want to endanger your star. You could arrange a reasonably good facsimile?"

"The right size, right dye job, right clothes, dark glasses, makeup, a quick study in the way she waves and walks. Sure. Ten minutes on the phone I've got one, believe me."

"But she gets maximum protection too."

"I would insist."

"Now here is the delicate point, Mr. Louker. If this Bogen is picked up, the cops are going to know the name he is using and the address he is using in about three minutes. Somebody has to be ready to move very quickly. At that address are going to be some things which should be destroyed, or maybe your star's career goes down the drain. Somebody has to be smart and quick."

"Are you going to give me more cramps?"

"Photographs, Herm. Of your star in a circus. A mob scene. If they got out it might not dent her too badly as long as she stays big at the box office. But two dog pictures in a row could cook her."

He got up and tiptoed about, patting his stomach, moaning softly. There was a lot of stomach. It started under his chin and descended in a long penguin curve to his knees.

"How can we get the pictures?" he demanded, more of himself than of me.

"Get a very nimble lawyer, and charge Bogen with stealing them from her. Get them impounded for her identification, then returned to her for destruction, and give him some impressive pieces of cash to hand out if he has to. Hell, you people have given out little gifts other times."

He studied me. "I know you from someplace, maybe? Like in Rome with Manny?"

"No."

"It will come to me. We'll work it out somehow." He took a wad of currency out and counted out a thousand dollars. "She said expenses. You can sign the receipt okay?"

I managed. He wished me well and left, looking gastric.

Dana wasn't very responsive the next morning. After I left

her room the head nurse on the floor intercepted me. She was wearing a curious expression, as if she had just discovered that if she flapped her arms hard enough, she could fly.

"Lysa Dean came to see her."

"Was she conscious then?"

"Oh no. Miss Dean was very shocked. She was very upset. I think she has a very warm heart."

"She must have."

"She left this for you, sir."

I opened it with one hand on my way down the hall. Heavy blue paper, scented. Sprawling backhand in blue ink. "I must see you. Please. L."

The cab took me there. The desk said sorry, she isn't registered here, sir. I gave them my name. Oh. Go right up, sir. She has the west wing on the fourth floor. A cop type guarded the wing. He glanced at the sling and spoke my last name with a question mark after it. Last door on the right, he said.

She sat on a dressing table bench in a white robe. A man was saying rude words over a phone. A thin man was fixing her hair. A girl in glasses was reading her a script aloud in a nasal monotonous voice. She shooed them all out.

"Dear McGee," she said. "Your poor arm, dear. Oh my God, the way Dana looked. It broke my heart. It really did. I actually wept."

"That's nice."

"Please don't be sullen. We're going to do what you suggested to Herm. They're going to fly a girl in. I'm going to hide out here like a thief, dear. God, things are going to get into the damnedest mess without Dana. They're going to pot already. How could she?"

"I guess it was just thoughtlessness."

She studied me, head cocked on the side. Then she laughed aloud. "Oh, no! Really? But when I kidded you in Miami, I never *really* thought you could actually *get* her. You must be very damned . . ."

"You would be doing me one of the world's greatest favors to please shut your mouth, Lee. There's been a lot of dying done. My shoulder aches. Dana is worth ten of you."

She went back and sat on the bench. "At least I know why you two were futzing around out here on my expense money. Making the fun last, eh?"

"That's right."

"Damn you, tell me the real reason."

"The man who took you for a hundred and twenty thousand was murdered. It looked as if M'Gruder might have done it and could be arrested for it sooner or later. Then that house party would have figured in the trial. I wanted to check it out."

The quick red fox stared at me with foxy eyes, instantly aware of the implications. She fingered her throat. "Off the hook on that, eh?"

"Yes. And I have a hunch you'll be in the clear on the other too. I wonder about you, Lee. Take a look at that house party list. Nancy Abbott is beyond hope. Vance and Patty and Sonny Catton are dead. The photographer is dead. Poor little Whippy is trade for the butch."

"Really? What is all this? The hand of God? Punishment? Don't be an ass, McGee. Sometimes the swingers go quicker. Maybe because they don't have their feet braced. If that kind of little fun-party could kill, honey, lower California would be shrinking. You know, you do drag a little. Have you noticed it? Oh, hell, I don't want to fight you. It's going to be weeks and weeks before Dana can get back on the ball. That's what they told me. I'll keep her on salary, of course. And there's a sick benefit thing she's entitled to. Scotty will check that all out for her and take care of it. I think . . ."

Herm came to the door and beckoned to her. She excused herself and went to him. They talked a few moments in low tones. He left and she came slowly back to me. "There's a meeting I don't dare miss. Damn it. I did want to see Dana, at least once more. Herm is going to have to smuggle me into town and bring the stand-in along later. McGee, my darling, I've got a thousand things to do . . ."

"You sent for me. Remember?"

She snapped her fingers. "Of course. Darling, you got the thousand expenses? You understand that our deal was to get me completely free and clear. Right? It's all or nothing, you understand. If your plan works, you come to see me and we'll settle up. All right? Darling, I do love Dana like a sister, but sick people depress me so. Could you find some nice little dude ranch or something for her, and a woman to take care. I'll have Victor Scott work out the money end with you. Would you mind terribly? After all, you *must* find each other attractive. I'm entirely clear publicity-wise on this end because, thank God, there isn't a shred to link me to Vance in any way." She patted my face. "Be a dear and take care of our girl. Give her my love, and bring her back to me when she's truly healthy again."

On Thursday afternoon the improvement in Dana was astonishing. The puffiness was gone, but there were saffron marks of the bruises. She wore lipstick. She was propped up. Her smile of greeting was shy.

They let me have an hour with her. She was anxious to know what had happened. I knew it might tire her, but I had to brief her before some official visited her and asked questions. I caught her up to date, including the plan to trap Bogen.

When I got back to The Hallmark at four that afternoon, there was a message to call a Los Angeles operator. When it went through, Lysa came on the phone, yapping with glee and relief. "McGee, darling? It worked, you shrewd, shrewd man! Our own people got him, and took away the nasty little gun he was going to shoot me with. Shoot the stand-in, I mean. And they went to his nasty little rooms and got all the photographs, and then they turned him and his nasty little gun over to the law. My God, I didn't even know the terrible tension I was under. It's *such* a relief."

"Wouldn't it be nice if you asked about Dana?"

"Give me *time*, for God's sake! All right. How is she?"

"Much, much better."

"That's fine. That's good to hear."

"You and I have a little accounting to do."

"I *know* that. Damn it, what makes you so sour? Give me a chance. What's today? Thursday. Let me look at my book." I waited five minutes and she came back on the line. "Darling, I'll be home Monday afternoon. You fly in and come talk to me about it."

"Talk to you about it?"

"Darling, you don't exactly have a contract, you know. And a frightened person can make some *very* rash promises. Technically, you really weren't in at the kill, were you?"

"Monday afternoon," I said and hung up. I did not know why I had been sour with her. Something was wrong, and I did not know what it was.

On Sunday afternoon I found out what my instincts had been trying to tell me. The nurse and I helped Dana into the wheelchair and I rolled her to the big sun room, to a private corner.

"Here's the way I have it lined up," I told her. I sat holding her hand. "Ten days before they spring you, then say a week or so more before you can travel, honey. So I tote you east, get you settled aboard, and after a few days we can go cruising. How does that sound?"

She gently, firmly pulled her hand away from mine. She looked away from me. "Travis, you have been very good to me."

"What's the matter?"

"It was all . . . mixed up and crazy. It wasn't me, really. I don't know how to tell you. I'm not like that. I'm married. I don't even know how I could have been so . . . so silly. I think it was because of working for her, maybe. I'm not going back to her."

I put my fingertips under her chin and turned her head and made her look at me. I looked at her until she flushed and twisted her head away. She meant it. A new conception. You could get a hit on the head that could knock love out of you for good and all. When their eyes go that dead for you, there's no way to ever get back. I knew what my instincts had been trying to tell me.

"You don't have to stay around," she said. "I mean, I'm used to looking after myself. I'll be fine, really. I do want to thank you for everything. I feel so sorry about . . . giving you the wrong idea and a lot of false hopes and . . ."

"You can still be honest, can't you?"

"Of course."

"How do you feel about my coming to see you here, Dana?"

She hesitated, then lifted her chin a half inch. "I d-dread it, Travis. I'm terribly sorry. It just keeps reminding me of something I'd rather forget."

Then all that was left us was the goodby ritual, which was, after the details of what to do with her belongings, and my promise to send a nurse to wheel her back to her room, a handshake. McGee, the great lover. This was one I wanted to keep. No, not this one. I didn't even know this one. The one I wanted to keep was the one Ullie had bashed on her way to go kill herself. This Dana wanted to forget that Dana. And damn well soon would. So shake hands with your darling and say goodby and try not to see the evident relief she tries to hide.

The cab deposited me in front of Lysa Dean's iron gates on Monday afternoon. The Korean let me through the gates. The maid let me into the house and then disappeared. The house was as silent as when I had been there with Dana. The big oil portraits of Lysa Dean stared emotionally at me through the half-gloom of draperied sunlight.

I roamed and plinked two notes out of the gold and white piano. Lysa Dean came swiftly into the room, in black knit pants and a white silk overblouse, an effective combination to go with gold-red hair in a room of whites and blacks and golds. She wore woolly white slippers and carried a white envelope in her hand. She hurried to me, stretched up to kiss me with the faked sweet-shyness of a welcoming child, and took me by my good hand to a vast couch in a shadowed alcove.

"How is dear Dana?" she asked.

"Marvelously improved."

"When can she come back to work, dear? I really need her, desperately."

"She'll have to take it easy for a while."

"McGee, darling, *do* use your influence on her. Tell her Lysa needs her *sooooo* much."

"I'll tell her that the very first chance I get."

"You *are* a huge old sweetie. Now what about the photos I gave you in Miami?"

"I've destroyed the ones I had made, with your face blanked out. When I get back, I'll destroy the other ones . . . unless you want them."

"God, I don't ever want to see them again. Darling, they say that little Bogen is way way off. If he'd tried to fire his rusty little gun, it would have blown his hand off. They are going to put him away."

"So now your life is all neatened up, Miss Dean. And you'll get to marry your dear friend. Congratulations. Is that my money you keep hanging onto?"

She handed me the envelope. I fumbled it open, and saw that it was light, and found that it counted up to ten thousand. It wouldn't count one inch past that. Before I could get the first word out, she was hanging onto me, laughing and teasing, saying, "Now darling, *do* be realistic, after all! I gave you all that nice travel money, and sent you off with quite a handsome and exciting gal, and you had some exciting and delicious adventures, all on the house. I'm really not *made* of money, darling. Taxes are fantastic. Really, when you think of it, I think you are doing terribly well out of this, and some of my advisors would think I was out of my head to give you all this." As she was talking she got the money out of my hand and slipped it into the inside pocket of my jacket, and was going quite directly and efficiently to work on me, with the quickness of a lot of little kissings, and an arching and presentation of all the celebrity curves and fragrances, a lot of cleverness of little hands, and a convincing steaminess of breath and growing excitement, worming her way astride my lap. This was the artist at work, at the work she knew best, operating from a life-long knowledge of the male animal, and quite convinced, apparently, that a good quick solid bang would send the man away too happy to care about being shorted, too dazed to object. Already she was beginning to work her way out of those soft knit pants and simultaneously beginning the little pressures which were supposed to topple me over onto my back on the big couch under a picture of the lady herself.

I got my good left arm in between us and my palm flat against her wishbone, then abruptly straightened my arm, sending her catapulting back, scrambling, slipping on the smooth hard terrazzo, sitting hard on a white furry rug and riding it back like a sled to end up under another picture so soulful the artist had indicated a halo effect.

She bounded up, hair masking one eye, yanking the knit pants up over the white behind. "What the hell!" she squalled. "Jesus Christ, McGee, you could have bust my tail bone!"

I was standing up, fixing my sling, starting toward the door.

"It's okay, Lee baby," I said. "I'll take the short count. You don't have to try to sweeten it. It wouldn't mean one damn thing to you, and it would mean just a little less than that to me."

I left amid a shrieking of ten-letter words, and I was hastened on my way by a hail of elephants. She had a collection. She threw fast, but not well.

I crunched down the finest grade of brown gravel, past

sprinkler water pattering on fat green leaves. The Korean let me out. I could feel the meager money-weight in my jacket pocket. I stopped and took my arm out of the sling and stuffed the sling in a pocket. The arm did not feel good swinging, so I tucked a thumb in my belt.

I walked and thought of what a weird way to lose a good woman. I saw old men carefully driving lookalike cars with names like Fury and Tempest and Dart. Through a fence I saw a quintet of little girls dashing in and out of the silvery spray of a sprinkler, shrilling. A dog smiled at me.

What a ridiculous way to lose a woman. They do not like pedestrians in that neighborhood. Polite cops stopped, asked polite questions, and politely drove me to the nearest taxi stand. I got into the cab and the only place to go was my hotel room, and I didn't want to go there, but I couldn't think of anything else.

When we stopped for a light I saw a magic store, and I asked the driver if he thought they might sell love potions in there. He said that if I was looking for action, just say the word. I went back to the hotel, and seventy minutes later I was on the Miami jet.